Iron Knights

~: honos ~ amicitia ~ fides :~

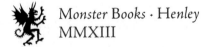

Monster Books · Henley
MMXIII

Iron Knights

~: *honos ~ amicitia ~ fides* :~

By
Robin Bennett

Iron Knights

(Aktuel Translations Ltd. *t/a* Monster Books)

Originally published in Great Britain by
Monster Books
The Old Smithy,
Henley-on-Thames,
OXON RG9 2AR

ISBN 97809568684-80
A catalogue record of this book is available from the British Library

Cover illustration
© Juan Darien via Fotalia

The text illustrations are adapted from Giff's original sketches, charcoal on birchbark, courtesy of the Four Frogs Cultural Heritage Centre.

*This book is dedicated
to the village of Four Frogs
and the hundreds just like it
dotted around England.*

*Thanks to Faye Newton
for all her hard work
and best of luck for the future.*

*Thank you to my 3 children:
Jude, Victor and Hortense
for all their enthusiastic input -
the good ideas and the raucous laughter
when anyone gets hit over the head
with a mace or falls down a well.*

*And thanks, as ever,
to my long-suffering wife, Helene,
who had to put up with all of this
nonsense at the dinner table and
on long car journeys.*

Heat up the Furnaces!

DESIGN YOUR OWN IRON KNIGHT COMPETITION

❧

Design your very own Iron Knight for the chance to win some serious pocket money.

Send us details of your version of an Iron Knight.
You can make it out of any material – it could be metal, wood, Lego, even an animation or a drawing! Dads (and mums) can help, especially if your Iron Knight needs the use of a blowtorch to create or carries a large axe.

So drag that suit of armour out of the attic (if you happen to live in a castle), nick the Lego back off your little sister, start mashing the papier mache or just sharpen your pencil and find a handy scroll.

➤ First prize £250 cash

➤ Second prize £150 cash

➤ Third prize £100 cash

The competition is open to anyone anywhere in the world and entry is free.

There are 3 easy ways to enter:

1 Email us your designs or clips (books@monsterbooks.co.uk)

2 or put them on our Facebook page (www.facebook.com/MonsterBooksUk) or

3 post your clips on YouTube (tell us where and we'll put them on the Monster Books Channel - MonsterBooksTV)

Then get all your friends and even some of your enemies to like and share on YouTube and Facebook!

Yes! This is not some feudal overlord type of competition, where we nobles (who can read) decide everything for you peasants. We'll very generously look at how many Facebook and Youtube likes you get.

We'll also look at

         ⇝ How much they remind us of the story

         ⇝ If they make us laugh (or **SCARE** our pants off).

Then a shortlist of twenty will be produced before Christmas and the casting vote will be in Jan 2014.

PART I
Rainbeard's Castle

❧

(Ages ago)

❧

(Hundreds of years at least)

CHAPTER I
~: *Four Frogs* :~

IT IS A UNIVERSAL LAW of nature that three boys let loose in any wood, in any part of the world, will get themselves into some sort of trouble before teatime.

'And so I says, "Ha ha, Soozie Brick, you'll never catch me and I don't care if I'm not wearing any trousers – or pants!" and that's why I ran into Gustus the Pig Herder, 'cos I was looking the other way, and so that's how he fell backwards and got stuck halfway down the well and Father Mally had to borrow that donkey – the one with the funny teeth – to pull him out … and anyway, it's a good thing he is *sooo* fat, otherwise he would have fallen all the way in and we'd have to go all the way to the river to get our water, 'cos you wouldn't want to drink anything Gustus had been in …'

All in all, Giff had the look of a boy who frequently found he had a lot of explaining to do.

At that moment, he was walking behind his much larger cousin, Venn, who strode on ahead, naturally taking the lead. With the same mop of blond hair and square build, the boys could have been mistaken for younger and older brother. The third boy, Pail – tall, dark and by far the quietest of the three – lagged behind, lost in his own thoughts.

It was mid-August and the woods were bathed in an eerie green light formed by the filtered sun chinking through the gently moving canopy of leaves above. The perfect weather, the mysterious feel of the woods and the fact that they had nothing much planned, all conspired to hint strongly at a wealth of possibilities before them that very afternoon.

Giff was so busy talking that he didn't notice Venn had

just stopped dead in his tracks. Bumping into Venn was a bit like walking into a small boulder. 'Ow! My dose!' grumbled Giff, rubbing his nose. 'Cheers …'

In response, Venn held up his hand, his whole body perfectly still. Tense. Giff stopped massaging his face for a moment and took an interest in what Venn was concentrating so intently upon. 'What is it?' he stage-whispered. There was a longish pause.

'Have you ever noticed that path before?' Venn murmured. Giff peered around his cousin. One fork in the path led down a familiar route that would eventually take them away from the woods and into some fields where there was an excellent trout lake. The other fork was a path he had to admit he'd never noticed before, although he'd been playing in these woods with his friends since he could walk.

Giff had been hoping that they were on their way to the lake – the thought of a freshly grilled fish, caught and cooked on an open fire, made his mouth start to water. On the other hand, the unexpected path was intriguing. It was so overgrown that it appeared as a green tunnel of thorns and bushes burrowing into the wood, further than the eye could see, and the nettles at its threshold seemed to be nodding gently as if to say, *yes, you are right boy, fascinating things are waiting this way.*

'Doesn't look like anyone's been down it for years,' remarked Pail, who'd only just caught up. A thought wrinkled his brow. 'Doesn't it lead in the general direction of the Castle?'

Now, this was important.

The boys all came from the same village, which was called Four Frogs. How a village came to have such an unusual name is a story for later but, for now, all you need to know is that the village of Four Frogs was small, quaint and largely ignored by the outside world – namely the rest of England.

The village, the tiny valley it nestled in, its fields and its woods; they were all owned by a moderately famous knight whom you might call eccentric if you were feeling generous, or borderline nuts if you were not.

Several generations before, the knight – whose name was Rainbeard – had left his castle to visit relatives in the wilds of the North, and he had not been seen by a soul since. In fact, so much time had passed that Granny Avfeldig was the only person still alive in the village who remembered him from when she was a small girl. And she was so old now; it looked like her skin was made of dry leaves and her hair cobwebs.

So, everyone assumed that Rainbeard was either dead or that he had simply forgotten all about them. This suited the humble inhabitants of Four Frogs because it meant that they were left alone to get on with their lives in peace. No-one bothered them much, and they bothered no-one back.

There was a Headman in the village, but there was only one rule. No-one, *under any circumstances*, was to step foot inside Rainbeard's Castle.

For ANY reason.

EVER.

✤

'Nah,' said Giff, 'the only way to the Castle is along the Ancients' Turnpike, past old Cobb's place, his dog chased us last time – remember, I had to hide in that mackerel barrel?'

'How could we forget,' replied Pail, gracing the world in general with a rare smile. 'After that, you were more popular than you've been in your whole life. I never knew that there were so many stray cats in Four Frogs.'

'Ha ha, how extremely hilarious you are, one day I'm sure I'll die of laughter talking to you,' replied Giff, 'but it wasn't me that screamed like a girl and ran up a tree …'

'I definitely think we should check this path out.' Venn still hadn't moved a muscle.

'Why?' asked Pail, who'd just remembered that sneaking past Cobb's place last time had been Venn's idea. In fact, when he considered it, most of their really dangerous adventures seemed to have Venn behind them, one way or another. Of course, Venn being Venn, he always had the most noble of intentions: either they were engaged in following a suspicious-looking traveller, or hunting for a lost pig, or something equally innocent and honourable. But somehow all his good intentions usually ended up with Pail or Giff getting into trouble.

'I don't like the look of it,' said Venn, who was glaring at the path as if it offended his sense of what was proper behaviour for a path with nothing to hide. 'Just seems like it might be a good idea to make sure it's not dangerous. Spies,' he added darkly, for no particular reason. 'And there might be something down there that the Headman needs to know about.'

'You mean *your dad*?' Giff was feeling a little tetchy – he was still thinking about grilled trout and fresh bread and he'd missed his afternoon snack – the one he always had just before tea, but after the one just after lunch.

'Well then,' said Pail, 'I say we explore it! We're not doing anything else, are we?'

Giff opened and shut his mouth a couple of times without saying anything. Between Venn's moral obligation to investigate anything and everything, and Pail, who would be the first to accuse him of being scared, he suddenly felt that fishing had gone off the afternoon's agenda. 'OK, let's go!' he said. 'Don't worry; I'll let you know if I see anything dodgy. Follow me!' But nobody heard him. Both his friends had sticks and were already some way ahead, slashing their way down the mysterious path.

High up in the branches of a beech tree, a beady pair of black eyes watched them disappear into the undergrowth.

❦

The sun seemed to freeze in the sky and all sound dulled as they made their way upwards through the dank and humid forest. Within half an hour, cutting through the thick bracken had lost its appeal. Giff was hot, tired and really, really hungry. Just as he was about to suggest they turn back and go fishing after all, the path widened and the brambles and other weeds clogging the way thinned out then disappeared altogether. Very soon, the three boys found themselves standing in a broad avenue of trees facing a stone arch that was slowly crumbling beneath the weight of green ivy and dog roses.

Giff was the first to speak. 'Well, we've never seen this before.'

'I'd say looks a bit *castle-like*,' remarked Pail, subtly proving a point both of his friends ignored. 'That's older than anything in the village.'

Venn seemed to be thinking as he approached one of the tottering pillars. He peered up at something under the archway. 'Pail?'

'Hmm?' Pail was squinting at the sun, trying to work out in which direction they had been going.

'Come and tell me what this says.' Apart from Venn's dad, Pail was the only other person in the village who could read. No-one had been able to work out how he had managed it, either – one day he had just picked up the old village Bible kept in the thatched chapel and had started to work out the letters, all by himself. Venn's dad had helped him out on some of the harder words but was amazed that by the end of the week Pail had read half of it on his own. And it was in Latin.

'Says what where?'

'Up there.'

Pail looked up at the dusty arch and saw that Venn was pointing at some lettering. 'No idea, it looks Greek to me.'

'At least give it a go, genius.' Giff stared up at the writing, his lips moving silently, as if he knew exactly what it said but was keeping it to himself for now.

Pail gave him a sour look down his long nose. 'No, I cannot. Like I said, it's Greek. It uses different lettering, that's all I know.'

Venn thought for a moment, then shrugged, as if it didn't make a difference anyway. 'OK, let's go on, this path must go somewhere …'

'Yeah,' said Pail. 'I worked out where we're heading, and sooner or later we'll end up somewhere around the east curtain wall of the Castle.'

Venn gave Pail his best reassuring smile and pushed his thatch of blond hair out of his face. 'Don't worry, Pail, we won't actually go in, I promise. Me, of all people, know that. But it's just a good idea if we check where this goes for sure – where's the harm in that?' He thumped Pail on the arm in a friendly way and grinned. 'Anyway, my dad may not know it exists or where it goes. If there is a secret road to the Castle and this is it, then he should be told about it. It's our duty.' Pail rubbed his arm and smiled back at his friend despite himself. Venn loved to sound like he was being noble.

'And of course the fact that it's pretty exciting and we're

bored has nothing to do with it.'

'An adventure!' Giff added happily.

As they carried on, they walked by something sticking out of the ground at an angle. Giff's leg brushed up against a creeper. He didn't notice the wooden sign it hid as he passed. *Keep out!* it said in plain English. *On pain of* **Pain**. *Trespassers will be eaten. Slowly. And digested. Poorly.*

Bit by bit, the avenue of trees they were traversing broadened out to make room for two streams – or at least channels of water – flowing either side of the path. 'That's odd,' remarked Pail, staring at them.

'What is?' Venn, still leading the way, turned his head slightly but kept walking.

'Well, one of those streams is flowing one way, back to the forest and the other one – this one,' Pail said, pointing with his stick to the stream on the right, 'is going the other way.'

'Oooh yeah, creepy,' said Giff, pulling a scary face, 'it's like it's following us … or *something*!'

Pail took a swipe at him with his stick but missed by a mile. 'I didn't say it was creepy, just a bit odd.' He paused, biting his lip thoughtfully. 'In fact, I think it's actually impossible. Two streams next to one another would have to flow the same way.'

'No they wouldn't,' replied Giff with all the authority he could summon, 'they can go whichever way they want – they don't have to listen to you.'

Pail rolled his eyes. 'OK, smart-arse, all water has to flow downhill. It's a fact – just like Venn's strong, I'm clever and you are an imbecile. So how can you explain why this one on the right is going up the hill?'

'Would you two stop arguing and come here?' Venn had disappeared around a corner shielded by trees.

Pail and Giff glared briefly at one another and followed

his voice. 'Crikey!' they both said at the same time as they rounded the corner.

The Castle walls rose up in front of them like a huge slab of cliff face. Everyone in Four Frogs had got used to seeing it from a distance, at the end of the valley, where it had always seemed as remote as the distant hills – all white and splendid. Not many other villages had their own castle, certainly none as big and generally magnificent as theirs, and they were proud of it. Unexpectedly close up, though, it was huge but less impressive: vines as thick as a man's leg twisted from the tangled undergrowth at the foot of the curtain wall, punching huge holes in the stonework. Other creepers clung on to the stone battlements, like the monstrous tentacles of a great sea creature that would one day decide to give a tremendous squeeze so that the whole Castle and its surrounding walls would crumble to mere rubble.

So, crikey about summed it up. None of the boys had seen another building even a tenth of the size before and, despite being a bit worse for wear, it was still imposing. An adder uncoiled itself from the foot of a creeper and slipped through a hole in the wall.

'Oh, well,' Giff said, 'now we've seen it, let's go.' Giff had a real problem with snakes and Pail knew it. Neither of the other two moved.

'Er, yes, er, of course,' said Venn vaguely, not taking his eyes off the enormous battlements. He looked a little troubled.

'Hmm,' said Pail and moved a bit closer, mainly because he knew it would upset Giff.

'C'mon guys – we shouldn't be here.'

'Well,' Pail seemed to be thinking, 'strictly speaking, the rule is no going inside the Castle. No-one said anything about looking at it from the outside. Technically, we do it every day.'

'Yes,' said Venn, brightening up a bit. 'We're going to have to report back to the Headman ...'

'You mean your dad ...'

'OK, yes ... *my dad*. So if we *do* stick around here, then we're just, um ... gathering information?' Venn looked at Pail for confirmation.

'What, hmm? Oh yeah, absolutely! Intelligence, you know ... if we report back on a secret path leading to the Castle, the details need to be ... er ... precise and ... um ... is it just me or is that bird giving us an odd look?'

'What bird?'

'That bird, up there.' Pail pointed at what looked like a large raven perched on the battlements. '*Revenus maxumus*, if I'm not mistaken.' Venn and Giff stared at it for a few moments. 'And I'm sure I saw it watching us earlier in the woods.'

'Well, Pail, I'm not sure, as I don't really make a habit of staring at big black birds ...' Venn started, but before he got much further, the raven swooped down and landed on a rock next to the three boys.

'Go away,' said Pail stuffily, 'obviously we're busy. And we've got no food.'

'Cark!' said the raven.

'Urgh!' said Pail, 'I hate their starey eyes and their wrinkly legs.'

'Buzz off,' said Giff, waving his stick about. 'I know an eagle.'

'Cark, cark,' replied the bird, making a sudden grab at something on Giff's belt.

'Hey!' shouted Giff; the raven darted away and flew back to the battlements. 'It's nicked my money pouch!'

'Maark, mark,' called the bird out of the side of its mouth, 'nah, nah, nah, naaah, nah!'

'Did that bird just say, *nah, nah, nah, naaah, nah?*'

asked Venn.

'I think so,' said Pail. 'Pretty impressive with its beak full.'

'Aarghh!' said Giff, jumping up and down on the spot. 'I can't believe it!'

Venn and Pail turned to stare at Giff. 'What on earth's wrong with you?' asked Pail, 'you've never got any money anyway.'

'No, you don't understand. My mum gave me all the family housekeeping money this morning to get some bread and eggs off old Ma Windy, *and* my brother gave me a penny to get some medicine off her.'

'What medicine would that be?'

'It calms him down. Well, basically stops him hitting people.' Giff's brother, Starl, had a huge body and a tiny head that resembled a frostbitten turnip. He was well known for losing his temper. The week before, he'd thrown Pail over a hedge just for breathing too loudly through his nostrils. He had claimed Pail was showing off.

'Whatever the medicine is, it doesn't work.' said Pail with real feeling.

'Believe me, he'd be a lot worse without it. He's going to kill me. Then my mum'll dig me up just so's my dad can kill me all over again. He loves his eggs in the morning and next door's baby needs milk.'

'Well, Giff, we'll certainly miss you when you are gone,' said Pail, looking to move off back the way they had just come.

'No, we've got to get my money back off the bird.'

Pail shook his head. 'No way, it's too risky.'

'Venn?' Giff turned to his cousin in appeal.

'Well …' Venn looked thoughtful, 'it's not your money, so you're not being selfish … and I guess we're not actually going inside the Castle if we just climb up to try and catch the bird.'

Pail shielded his eyes. 'Well, whatever we decide to do, we should do it quickly before it decides to fly off.'

'Come on then,' said Venn, grabbing a creeper and hauling himself up, 'the sooner we get this over with, the better.'

'Thanks guys,' said Giff in real relief, 'I owe you one.'

CHAPTER 2
~: Joust :~

FIFTY MILES AWAY, in the grounds of quite a different castle, hundreds of people from all walks of life were gathered for *The Croxe Castle Annual Joust, Alarmingly Big Vegetable Growing Competition and Garden Fete.*

'Boiled sheep's eyes, get your boiled sheep's eyes here – fresh last January … still squidgy!' The food seller was standing right outside Sir Godfrey's tent. He was shouting so loudly that poor Sir Godfrey was having trouble remembering what bit of his armour went where. 'Intestines, lurverly intestines, it may be offal but we love it! Dried toad on a stick!'

It's all junk food at these things nowadays, thought Sir Godfrey, shaking his head. He had just muddled up his breastplate with his backplate and his chain mail was inside out, so he decided to take it all off and start again from the bottom. Right! Sabatons on his feet, with greaves and cuisses to protect his legs from people poking swords at them; revebecces and vambraces, strapped onto his arms by his servant, young Tom, who was actually just the cook's son, and was doing his best, poor chap. These were followed by his gauntlets with gadlings – these being rather nasty-looking spikes – on the knuckles. Sir Godfrey, who was a nice old fellow, couldn't actually imagine gouging someone's eyes out with them, but he did often find them rather useful for weeding the difficult bits between the stones in the garden. Finally, large breastplate on the front, backplate and faulds – reinforced plates that stopped a lance going right through you like a kebab stick.

'Nearly there!' he puffed, trying to sound more cheerful

than he felt. Tom kept on tripping over Sir Godfrey's lance. It was over fourteen feet long and took up a lot of room in the small tent. 'Help me with my sword belt, there's a good chap.' Tom picked up the belt and strapped it on as best he could, whilst Godfrey looked at the choice of swords. The giant broadsword looked a lot like hard work, but the falchion was definitely too short and a bit weedy looking – really not much good against a heavily armed knight carrying a colossal axe – but then again, what was? 'I'll take the bastard sword, that one there ...' he grunted with the effort of pointing, '... in the middle.' It was his favourite; he'd had it since he was a young squire, learning how to be a knight from his father, Sir John the Bald. He liked it because it was light enough to be used one-handed but was big enough to make a good dent on someone's helmet. 'On second thoughts, I'll have that mace too.' Horrible thing, but it balanced him out and stopped him falling over sideways when he turned.

Helmet, straps, shield with the Larkspur coat of arms – supposedly a lion on its hindquarters looking fierce but actually it looked a bit like a domestic cat waving – and their family motto underneath – *Semper Pronto* – meaning *always ready*, which everyone who knew Sir Godfrey found extremely funny.

Right, that was it. He was finally all set to go out, get on his horse and face all the other knights. Sir Godfrey Larkspur, of proud and noble lineage, stood up slowly and turned towards the door. He paused. 'Tom?'

'Yes, Sir Godfrey.'

'Have you grown recently?'

'When was that, Sir?'

'Oh, in about the last five minutes.'

'Urr, no, Sir, I don't think so, Sir. I'm sorry, Sir, if I 'ave.'

Godfrey looked down at his legs. It had been raining over

the past few days and the ground was soggy. Sir Godfrey sighed. He was slowly sinking into the mud, which had already reached his knees. He was stuck.

'I'm getting too old for this,' he said to no-one in particular.

CHAPTER 3
~: *Castle* :~

BACK AT THE DESERTED CASTLE, the
three boys had started to climb the
curtain wall.

It took them about ten minutes of hard
grappling, hand over hand, to hoist
themselves up and over the parapet.
Amazingly, it was Giff who got to the top
first. 'Right, where's that thieving bundle of
greasy black feathers?'

'Steady,' said Venn, 'don't just go charging after
it, we don't want it to fly off again.' However, the
bird in question showed very little sign of going anywhere.
As the friends had made their way up the ivy, it had taken
the precaution of hopping a few feet away along the wall,
but other than that it had stayed close. Now it was blowing
raspberries.

'How's it doing that?' asked Pail, finally getting to the top.

'No idea,' said Venn. 'Dad says Rainbeard left a lot of
strange things hanging about the Castle when he went away,
that's probably why we're forbidden to come here. I guess
this might be one of them.'

'Granny Avfeldig told my mum that he used to fly about
the Castle on this great big wooden bird and that he had
this box that talked with the voices of people from miles
away. She says that he's not a knight at all but a warlock.'

'A war-what?'

'It's a magician, but not the sort you would want turning
up at your birthday party.'

'Well, a raven that can blow raspberries with its mouth

full of money must be one of his crowning achievements, I imagine,' observed Pail. He turned to watch Giff edging down the wall towards the raven, who hopped away a few feet. Eventually, Giff lost his temper and threw a stone at it.

'Caark!' said the raven and flew off. Giff threw a larger rock at its retreating form, missing by several yards, and swore.

Pail shook his head before looking around. 'This place is huge.'

'It's big enough to house an army and at least ten villages,' agreed Venn. 'What I don't understand is why Rainbeard needed all this space. It's not like he had a large family.'

'I think he built it for us,' said Pail, 'in case we needed safety.' Venn looked doubtful. 'Then why aren't we allowed in?'

'Well, first of all that law has always seemed odd to me,' said Pail. Then he saw the look on Venn's face. 'No, seriously. Who made that rule up? I don't think Rainbeard did … I think it was something we just sort of decided after he left.'

'Hmm, well,' Venn looked like he didn't agree, 'it's for our own good. Can you imagine the likes of Starl being allowed to wander around here with all this magic and stuff?'

'What magic? All we've seen so far is a stream that might be flowing the wrong way and a bird that can do impersonations and who's a total thief – not more unusual than a magpie.'

'I dunno,' Venn shook his head, 'places are usually empty for a reason. And this place is suspicious.' He pointed up at the looming building at the end of the courtyard. His father referred to it as the Fast Tower. 'Don't you get the feeling that we're being watched from one of those dark windows? Makes you feel funny.'

'GUYS!' Giff was jumping up and down on the spot again, 'there's nothing funny about what's going to happen to me if I don't get that purse back.'

'OK, OK,' said Venn, 'but we've got to use our heads now. Look, he's up there by that window in the tower. We need to make him come to us. Have you got any food on you, Giff?'

'Silly question,' said Pail.

The boys moved closer to the main building.

Creepers and the rest of the forest hadn't penetrated the inner courtyard yet. The stone flags were a myriad of colours in highly polished marble: swirls of red and pink, deep blue and dark chocolate.

'Those look almost edible,' remarked Giff.

'I wonder where Rainbeard got the stone from? It doesn't look like anything from around here.' Pail was always more practical.

Venn walked around the base of the tower, prodding the stones with the stick he was still carrying. The Fast Tower rose up above where they stood, twice the height of the tallest tree in Four Frogs, tapering to a point at the end, like a giant needle. An old wooden staircase wound around the base of the tower, corkscrewing up the outside wall until it reached a small opening right at the very top where the raven now marched up and down self-importantly, jiggling the purse in its beak. 'It's almost like it wants us to go in,' Venn mused.

'That occurred to me too … but what choice do we have?' Pail added quickly, when he saw the look on Giff's face. 'I don't like the look of those stairs though.' All three studied the tall staircase with its rotting boards and missing steps. To Pail, it even looked like it swayed gently in the wind.

'Yeah, but I can't see another way up,' said Venn.

'Won't that ghastly bird just fly off, even if we do manage to get up there without breaking our necks?' Pail had gone a little pale – perhaps it wasn't worth the risk after all.

But Venn had got the bit between his teeth. 'No way, that bird is a thief and needs to be taught a lesson. Besides, we're brighter than him.'

'I wouldn't count on it.'

'Well, you are anyway … and we've got almonds. We'll use your cunning and Giff's nuts!'

Behind him, Pail rolled his eyes.

With that, Venn stepped forward and put a foot confidently on the first step.

It instantly reduced to dust. There was a pause, then a loud creaking noise as the rest of the staircase fell away from the wall, smashing to dry splinters with a tremendous crash. It would have killed Giff, if he hadn't dived under a stone bench at the last second. Slowly, the dust settled. 'I think we're going to have to find another way in,' said Pail, brushing the splinters out of his hair.

High up in the Fast Tower, something cold and seemingly lifeless awoke at the sound of the outer staircase falling away. It was weak, almost to the point of lifelessness. The raven had been its last chance.

Ahh,

　　p r e y .

🦋

CHAPTER 4

~: Joust :~
· Part Two ·

BACK IN THEIR TENT, Tom had just managed to pull Sir Godfrey free of the mud. They were both filthy and exhausted and the wretched tournament hadn't even begun.

Feeling sorry for his master, whom he liked, Tom began the laborious task of cleaning the armour with whatever rags came to hand. The armour had belonged to Godfrey's great-grandfather, Sir Brian Larkspur, the old king's favourite, but it had seen better days – dents, riveted plates to cover rents in the armour and rust spots all had to be scraped and polished so he looked his best and didn't embarrass himself in front of all the other knights.

Luckily, this was a small tournament and most of the other combatants were also wearing hand-me-downs that were the wrong size or last century's fashion. Armour was expensive and, given the choice between a spanking new suit of chain mail or food over the winter for everyone from the scullery maid upwards, Sir Godfrey wouldn't hesitate. Unlike some. Tom knew he was lucky to have a kind master and so he didn't mind helping out.

Jousting he just didn't get, though. Why would anyone would want to travel fifty miles to spend all afternoon putting on a metal coffin, then get on a horse, only to be knocked off it again a few minutes later by some toff with more money than sense? It was beyond him – but that was nobles for you. Too much time on their hands.

He looked out of the tent at Croxe Castle itself, nestling a little way up the hill, its pennants flapping red, gold and green in the breeze. The sight of small children splashing about in the shallow moat, innocently laughing, reminded him of when he used to come with his mum. He gazed at green fields beyond the castle, at the cattle gently grazing their way along the river and the willows.

Nice day for it though, he thought.

❧

Finally, waddling out of his tent, trying to remember where he parked his horse, Sir Godfrey saw a familiar face. 'Frobisher!' he cried at a tall, thin Knight in enormous spectacles. 'You jousting in this afternoon's card?' His old friend turned around, his rusty armour making an awful dry, scraping noise. Even compared to Sir Godfrey's, it was in a terrible state: over two hundred years old and it seemed to have spent most of that time at the bottom of a lake.

'Yes,' he said lugubriously, 'briefly, I hope.'

Old Frobisher was possibly the scruffiest knight in the whole of England – looking at his rusting, battered armour, Godfrey felt a bit better about his own suit.

Unlike Sir Godfrey, though, Lord Frobisher had pots of cash and a huge, crumbling castle in Wessex called Eruditas, which leaked and creaked but somehow never quite fell down. He chose to spend most of his money on books, which were even more expensive than weapons. Still, each to his own.

'Good, perhaps we can keep each other company on the journey home?'

'Hmm,' said Frobisher, 'yes, why not?'

Papapa papapapapaaaa pah! Horns sounded from the enclosure.

'Ah, well, looks like we're up.'

'Yes, I suppose so … worse luck.'

Frobisher's squire, a small lad named Simkin with frizzy

hair and a keen expression, ran over. He was very red in the face. 'My Lord, my Lord, we have to hurry, that was our call!' He was carrying a battered shield with the Frobisher coat of arms – a scroll with the words *bonus libri, canis, incendia*[1] – and a huge lance that looked as if it had been carved out of solid mahogany from a ship's mast. It must have been like trying to lift a medium-sized tree.

Frobisher glared at his squire who, in his opinion, was far too keen on jousting. 'I know, Simkin, I'm not deaf.'

'Of course not, my Lord. My Lord?'

'Yes, what is it now?' Frobisher had got his long legs caught up in someone else's tent rope and was having some trouble not falling over.

'There's a sale on at Prodd & Jabbe. New elm lances, light as a feather, strong as a beam. Ten percent longer for no extra cost – and there's a free pilgrimage up for grabs with every purchase.'

'Don't be an ass, Simkin, no-one ever wins those pilgrimages and, anyway, what do I need a new lance for?' Frobisher looked mystified.

'Well, um …' Simkin looked at Sir Godfrey for assistance, but he was staying well out of it by pretending to enter the *Knighte who looketh most like his Horse* competition. Simkin's shoulders slumped in defeat. 'Nothing, Sire.'

'Quite so, come on then, look lively! I think we left Miss Molly in a paddock over that way somewhere.'

They walked towards the field where about twenty horses grazed under the watchful eye of several small children. Vendors were out in force, their stalls selling everything a knight and his family could possibly want. Amongst the homemade cakes, woolly hats and exotic jewellery stalls was a shifty looking man standing by a tree. He held something

---

[1] Good book, dog, warm fire

forlorn on a short, frayed lead. Sir Godfrey was intrigued. 'What have we here, Sir?' he enquired, peering through a gap in his visor.

'Genuine dragon, Squire,' said the man tapping a sign nailed to a tree that said **Dragonne, veri fierce**. 'Ideal guard. Good with children.'

'It's a big lizard,' said Frobisher shooting the man a withering glare. 'Probably got it off one of those Moorish traders. Poor animal.' The shifty man seemed to shrivel a bit under Frobisher's gaze, but rallied.

'It's just a baby, your lordship, but fully grown it will be the perfect addition to the modern castle. Anyone trying to rob you will be roasted, all you'll need is a dustpan and brush in the mornin' – make the neighbours jealous. And terrified out of their wits,' he added after a moment's hesitation.

Before Frobisher could come up with a suitably sarcastic reply, they heard a familiar voice from a large tent nearby. 'There you chaps are! I was beginning to think you'd been attacked by bandits, ha, ha, ha!' Both knights turned awkwardly around in their respective armours to look at a rather portly man standing under a painted sign that showed a pig with a huge grin on its face (if that can be imagined). The *Happy Hog Inn* was a permanent fixture at the *Croxe Annual Joust, etcetera … and Garden Fete.*

'Ah, Locke, not taking part?' asked Sir Godfrey, clanking over.

"Fraid not, doctor's orders – strained a muscle in my stomach, too much sword practice, I think.'

'Too much eating, I think.' muttered Frobisher just loud enough for their old friend Percival Locke – honourable Knighte of Glamorgan – to hear.

'I say, is that dung on your armour, ha, ha, ha?'

'No, mud,' replied Sir Godfrey rather uncomfortably. He'd actually been wondering the same thing since Tom had pulled him out – there was an evil smell coming from somewhere close by. 'Anyway,' he said quickly, just to change the subject, 'we're probably going to bow out early – give these younger chaps have a chance, what?'

'Absolutely,' agreed Percival solemnly. 'But not before you've shown them a thing or two. I expect that sword arm of yours is twitching to enter the fray, what? To hew and cleave? Ha!'

If by twitching he meant a dull ache because Tom had tied the leather straps too tight, then yes, thought Godfrey unhappily, he supposed so. They began to move off.

'Are you coming Locke?' asked Frobisher, 'or are you just going to stand there gassing like an imbecile?'

'Oh, I think I'll stay here and gas,' replied Percival good-naturedly. If Percival was upset by anything Frobisher ever said, he hadn't shown it in the almost half a century that they had been friends. 'Bit peckish, have to keep my strength up for the return journey. Plus the sight of you chaps having fun and showing knights twice your size and half your age how it's done will be too much to bear, I fear.'

'Just as you like, we'll be off then,' said Sir Godfrey. 'See you in an hour.' Tom and Simkin were coming back with the horses.

'Break a leg!'

Frobisher nodded. 'Quite probably.'

CHAPTER 5

~: Deserted :~

PLAN B.

The boys now stood on the threshold of a stone-arched doorway. They had discovered it at the far end of the courtyard after the staircase leading up the tower had collapsed so spectacularly and it seemed to be the main entrance to the castle. The door itself hung open on its hinges and leaves had blown inside, gathering in corners of the vast entrance hall.

From where they stood, the hall looked bare, save for cobwebs that hung from rafters in thick clumps and a large mirror propped up against the far wall. Although it was old and very dusty, the boys could clearly make out the reflection of nothing like what was actually in the room they were looking at. Instead, the mirror showed an alleyway of twisted trees at night and what looked like a tall stone tower at its end. At the top of the tower, a window glowed with faint candlelight and a dark figure could just be made out.

The shrouded silhouette of a man seemed to be watching them.

'Wow!' said all three boys at once.

'Now that is scary,' said Giff.

'Cark!' The raven appeared at the top of a long, sloping flight of stairs, where it perched with Giff's pouch still in its beak.

'OK,' said Venn, voicing what they all wanted to hear, 'we go in, get Giff's money, get out.'

'OK, let's split up,' suggested Giff.

'Great idea, that way we can get in three times as much trouble.'

'We don't stop to look around, we don't touch anything and, most important of all,' Venn glanced at Giff, 'we stick together.'

'Agreed,' said Pail.

'Right,' said Giff, 'fine by me.' And with that, the first villager of Four Frogs in nearly a hundred years stepped over the threshold and into Rainbeard's Castle.

❧

Warm, musty air from somewhere deep within blew without as they crept up the staircase to the first landing. To the boys, the castle was so huge on the inside, they might as well have still been outside. By the time they got to the top of the stairs, the raven was disappearing at the end of a very long corridor in a series of hops and struts. Several doors could be seen along the landing, all closed, bar one. 'Quick,' said Giff, pointing along the corridor. 'Down here!'

'I think we can all basically agree now that the bird is leading us somewhere?' asked Pail.

'Yes,' agreed Venn. 'But we don't have much choice if we want the money back.'

'Don't be stupid,' said Giff, who was already half way down the corridor. 'It's just a b*iiiirrrrrdddd*! Aaaargh!' A hook, like a sort of one-fingered claw, shot out of the open doorway and grabbed Giff by the collar, pulling him sideways and out of sight.

The other two boys rushed forward. 'Giff!' shouted Venn, but before he could get to the door, it closed with a loud creak and a thud.

'Giff, you idiot, stop mucking around!' Pail looked around the edges of the doorframe, trying to spot a gap. There was no response from Giff.

'What's this?' Venn was fiddling with something beside

the doorframe.

Pail turned around quickly, but before he was able to remind Venn of his own advice not to touch anything, Venn gave the lever a pull. Instantly, two more hooks came down from the ceiling, catching Venn by his trouser belt, pulling him upwards. Pail just had time to see Venn's legs waving about as he disappeared into a funnel hanging from the ceiling. Quite alone now, he was left looking up and down the empty corridor.

'Oh deary me,' he thought. 'So much for not splitting up.'

Chapter 6
~: *Harp Stairs* :~

Pail was just wondering what to do next when he heard the now-familiar clickety-clack of claws on polished floor.

'Cark! Tut!' The bird gave him an impatient look and disappeared again around the corner.

Pail hesitated – he didn't like or trust the bird, but he really had no better ideas. He shrugged and followed.

The deserted corridor twisted this way and that for what seemed like a very long time, the raven hopping and strutting, keeping a few metres ahead of him, stopping once in a while to allow him to catch up. Just when Pail was quite seriously wondering to himself if these endless corridors were ever going to end, they did. Coming to a small archway, the raven uttered a relieved cry and took to the air.

Pail caught up and opened his mouth to gawp at the yawning empty space that was apparently the echoing inside of the Fast Tower. Out of all the huge indoor spaces Pail had experienced in the last hour or so, this dwarfed the lot. *Roomy* was clearly something that Rainbeard had taken to heart when designing and subsequently furnishing the Castle.

As with the rest of the place, the interior of the Fast Tower was empty of furniture, old and dusty. There was only one staircase, each step held up by a long wire that ran all the way to the ceiling, high above. The stairs led up to a door that was just visible at the top of the tower.

Pail looked around. The raven had disappeared somewhere all the way up there so he sighed and put a foot on the first step. *DOWH!* A noise like a giant harp being plucked rang out. Pail started, inadvertently placing a second foot on the next step. *RAAA'yyyy!* The wires holding the step hummed and vibrated, creating a not-unpleasant noise that reverberated around the empty space. It's got perfect acoustics thought Pail, thinking, with regret, of their own cramped chapel in the village.

'Hellooo,' he suddenly heard a small voice from higher up. 'Is there anyone there?' Up until now, he hadn't noticed the small windows that were carved at intervals through the thick, stone walls of the tower. 'I'm upside down and I need to wee!' It was Giff. Naturally.

'I'm here too! Now, if I can just chew through this wire …' That was Venn, who appeared to be much higher up – his voice echoed from outside the window, almost at the very top. Pail raced up the steps.

Meefaaa'soo, laaa, tee, dowwwh!

Pail poked his head out of the first window he reached and was rewarded with the sight of Giff's buttocks. The hooks that had grabbed him were apparently attached to a pulley that hung outside the castle. Pail smiled. 'Lucky I came along,' he said crossly, to hide his pleasure at seeing Giff safe and well. 'If I hadn't found you, you'd have been stuck there for good! Or until Rainbeard gets back, which, given we were responsible for smashing his staircase outside, I hope is never.'

'Can you get me down?'

Pail raised an eyebrow. 'Possibly, if you think I'm going to sprout wings anytime very soon.'

Giff hung there for a moment, frowning. 'No,' he said eventually, having given it serious thought. 'I don't.'

'Didn't think so,' said Pail. 'In that case you'll have to stay put for now.'

Giff started wriggling about. 'Fine,' he began, 'I'll sort myself out.' Just then something snapped.

Giff dropped. 'Aaargh!' On instinct, Pail grabbed at him, catching hold of his wrist by some fluke. Unfortunately, he was off balance, and Giff's weight instantly dragged him over the windowsill. Just as Pail felt sure he would be yanked all the way over, leading to both of them being turned into strawberry jam substitute, far below on the stone flags, something snagged.

Pail and Giff hung there for a few moments with nothing but the hem of Pail's underwear caught on an old nail to keep them from tumbling to certain death. In spite of being terrified, Pail mustered up as much disdain as he could manage, whilst hanging upside down. 'This is entirely your fault,' he hissed.

At that moment, he felt strong hands grab his waist and haul him in.

'In you get,' said Venn, 'and stop mucking about, we've still got to find that bird!'

'That was *brilliant*, best fun I've had in ages!' exclaimed Giff, rather spoiling the whole effect of being saved, grinning broadly as he climbed back inside. 'Those hook things pulled me through all these tunnels really fast ... then *you* turned up and starting being all snotty, then the wire snapped and I was all like, "help, save me!" and you grabbed hold of me, but then you fell too, and you were all like, "when we get out of this I'm going to kill you", just like in the stories ... except I knew you didn't mean it, you were enjoying it as much as me ...'

Pail looked daggers at Giff, only just resisting the urge to shove him back out of the window.

'Um, guys, when you've finished chatting, you ought to come up here and take a look at this.' Pail and Giff turned around and looked up the giant, harp-like staircase. Venn's voice was coming from behind the door at the very top of the stairs.

'Venn!' shouted Giff.

'Hurry up you two, that bloody bird's up here. It's still got your purse, but I can't catch it on my own.'

'No problem, I'm coming!' shouted Giff. He pushed past Pail and dashed up the stairs. Pail sighed and followed.

Both the boys, running at different speeds, rather spoiled the effect of the musical scales but Giff hardly seemed to notice as he got to the top of the tower and burst through the door, gasping for air. Pail ran in after him and was pleased to see they were in a big but very messy circular room at the very top of the Fast Tower. The floor was solid stone and he was especially pleased about that, too – the stairs had started to make him feel a bit giddy. Swaying about, hundreds of feet up in the air, with no barrier between them and the edge – that might have been Giff's idea of fun, but it was definitely not Pail's.

In the middle, settled on a table covered in dusty parchments, was the raven. It gave the newcomers a beady glare and ruffled its feathers.

Venn, who was looking slightly dishevelled after his own ride, seemed to be trying to creep around the back of it. Giff did a little sort of jig, waving his arms about frantically. 'Don't get any closer!' he squeaked at his cousin, slightly hysterically, 'it looks like it's going to fly off again.'

'Don't worry,' said Venn. 'Now we've got it surrounded.'

'Naaark!' said the raven, and dropped the purse on the table. The instant it did so, something about the bird seemed to change. It seemed to become somehow more birdlike, if that was possible and it definitely seemed surprised to find itself in the dusty, circular room. 'Caaark, caaark CAAARK!' it screeched loudly, making all three jump back in shock.

Venn was the first to recover. He dived at the bird, but missed, ending up sprawled across the table. With a flutter of its wings, the raven flew up towards the window, cuffing Venn across the head as it went. It stopped, perching on the ledge for an instant, before it hopped over the edge with a final indignant squawk and soared away.

'Got it!' exclaimed Giff, holding the purse triumphantly as if he'd done it all by himself. 'Don't mess with Giff again!' he shouted at the empty window, waving his retrieved purse. 'And you'd better not have spent anything.'

'Well, that certainly told him,' remarked Pail sarcastically, marching over to the window to get a closer look at a large cylindrical object, balanced on three stilts. He looked down the tube, but immediately started back, looking round each side of it in confusion before peering down the tube once more – gingerly at first, then with growing interest. 'This is amazing!' he said, 'everything looks bigger ... you can see the whole village from here ... I can see your dad, Giff ... urgh, he's scratching his –'

'But!' interrupted Venn, 'I'm guessing that you two might want to see this first.' He had moved over to the far side of the room where a space had been cleared in the mess of papers, stuffed animals and jars of things. In the corner were three very large dustsheets and Venn had his head under one.

'What is it?' asked Giff, who was pleased to change the subject from what his dad may or may not have been scratching. Venn didn't answer at once; instead, his friends heard him rap his knuckles on something that sounded big, metallic and hollow. He stepped back, the dustsheet falling away from his excited face, and pulled a corner of the material as hard as he could.

※

Later in life, on cold nights by the fireside, Giff would tell his grandchildren that his first sight of the Iron Knights had been the changing point in his life – that he'd known the very moment he laid eyes on them that he was looking at something powerful, something mysterious, something extra special. The truth was, in fact, far simpler, though no less dramatic: instantly, and without any discussion, all three boys decided that they had never – even in their imaginations – seen anything so cool.

'Wow!' said Giff who had never clapped eyes on a whole suit of armour in his life, let alone three at once. Venn stood grinning like all his birthdays had just arrived at the same time, whilst Pail gave a low whistle, which, for him, was the equivalent of doing cartwheels around the room and then doing the Can-Can in a pair of frilly knickers.

Just then …

Pail shook his head – surely the index finger of the largest knight hadn't just moved. He must have imagined it because, despite the dustsheets, all three figures were incredibly dirty, their metal joints stuck fast with grime and rust.

The suit nearest Venn was the smallest – although it was far larger than a normal man – being about seven foot at the very least, Pail guessed. And the armour looked like nothing he had ever seen before (not that he had ever had much time to study a real knight close up but, unlike Giff, he had seen brightly painted illustrations in books and some old parchments lying about the church). From where he stood, the suit appeared to have a series of sharp spines running down the back of the breastplate and along the shoulders and arms. The armour's feet were long and pointed; they looked almost as sharp as needles where they tapered to vicious points at the tips. Most extraordinary of all, the helmet's visor was also pointed and slightly curved, like the beak of a snipe or woodcock. In fact, the whole ensemble reminded Pail of a rather cross, dangerous-looking bird. In his head, he nicknamed it Squawk.

The second suit of armour stood about half a foot taller and carried what he knew to be a mace: a long baton of metal topped with a jagged, seven-pointed star of heavy lead. One direct hit from that would stop a bull in its tracks, let alone a knight, even if he were wearing the best helmet ever made. The suit seemed to have been designed for someone extremely thick-set – broad shouldered and very deep, it was standing there slightly bow-legged like a troll: large, dense and thoroughly brutish. The suit had extra bulbous extensions to the plate metal, almost as if it needed extra room for meaty arms and knotted muscles. Pail, who instinctively categorised anything new he came across, decided Bludge would be a good name for it.

The third, the tallest, had no adornments at all, just a long, slender sword. In spite of this, it managed to look the most menacing of all. The visor was firmly closed, black and blank-looking, with just the narrowest of slits for the eyes. From its stance, it seemed to be facing the window, as if searching for something beyond the curtain wall of the castle deep in the woods. Pail fancied it could have watched them (if it were alive) as they crossed the courtyard earlier. Even though he was still hot from his climb, he felt himself shiver. 'I name you Bane,' he murmured.

Despite all three being very different in shape, they were definitely part of a set. Underneath the dirt of decades, each was the same deep black, the only relief being gold trim that ran along the joins or folds in the armour and a gold crest that furled out from Bane's helmet, like a small crown. The gold still shone out in the relative gloom of the room and, to Pail, served to make the black metalwork all the darker and deeper.

Pail edged closer and inspected the armour carefully, and he noticed some writing – something embossed in the plate armour of each, along the thigh protection. *Iron Knight*, the stamp said, (*this way up*). *Chivalry not included. Work ~ power ~ service.* Hmm, thought Pail.

'They're suits of armour for giants!' was Giff's first opinion.

'Not exactly giants,' replied Venn staring up at them, 'but definitely the biggest human beings I've ever seen.' He went over and rapped his knuckle again on Squawk's breastplate. It sounded surprisingly solid to the boys.

'That's strange,' remarked Pail, voicing what they were all thinking. He tried pulling the mace but Bludge seemed to have it in a rigid grasp. 'Real suits of armour can't actually grab things,' he remarked, 'they're just held together with bits of wire and string.'

'Um,' said Giff, walking around the back of Bane. 'What's this do, I wonder?'

Oh no! thought Pail. But before he could stop him, Giff had pressed something under Bane's arm. There was a click and a grating noise of metal on metal as the front of Bane's breastplate fell open. Just then, the sun re-appeared from behind a small white cloud, and a bright shaft of light illuminated the knight's torso.

The boys blinked at the unexpected presence inside the knight: instead of an empty space filled with dust and cobwebs (and perhaps the odd spider), its chest contained rusted cogs and wheels, connected together with pulleys and minute spindles. The sun shone through these intricate works, and where Bane's heart would have been (had an Iron Knight need of one) something sparkled back menacingly – deep red – a large rock crystal that could only have been one thing: a ruby the size of an apple.

Venn, for once, was first to break the silence. 'What on earth,' he said, 'have we found?'

CHAPTER 7

~: Joust :~
·Part Three·

FOR THE TIME BEING, we must leave the boys and their intriguing discovery to return to Sir Godfrey and Frobisher. On the face of it, things weren't going well. Not well at all.

First of all, Frobisher was immediately disqualified from the tournament for forgetting his shield and helmet. His opponent, a nervous Knight called Pleek, went through to the next round, looking terrified and more than a little queasy. But Frobisher brightened up no end when he saw who Godfrey had drawn. By now, Percival had torn himself away from the delights of the Happy Hog and had ambled down to the arena to lean over the fence where Godfrey sat on Clover. 'Looks like you've got old Gaunt down the other end, ha!' he said pointing a half-chewed chicken leg at a huge knight in grey scale armour. 'Lucky chap! What I'd give to test my strength against a real opponent like him – fearsome reputation, even in friendly jousts – I heard he hit Lord Farquar at last year's tournament so hard with that morning star of his, the poor man still can't get his helmet off. Apparently, he also thinks he's a bell; only thing he'll say is "bong!" His wife, Lady Farquar, insists it's an improvement all-round. But sadly, for me …' He shook his head, as if the disappointment of not being able to fight the maniac down the other end was too much to bear.

From about a hundred yards away, Gaunt's horse, a gleaming grey stallion in brand new armour that matched his master's, pawed the ground and snorted. Sir Godfrey's own horse, Clover, shivered and backed away.

'Yes, absolutely.' Sir Godfrey was glad his visor was closed.

That way no-one could see his teeth chattering.

Paa p'pa pa pa pa paaa pah!!! The trumpets sounded again as a man in tights and a large floppy hat strode into the arena.

'A H E M ! My Lords, ladies and common villains … In the red corner, wearing … ooh, a lovely suit of armour in slimming grey, sooo this season, drop-waisted … coat of arms, the famous coiled viper *rampant*, sporting the motto, *No Quarter* … his Excellency, the Duke of Danger, the Lord of the Sword, the Mighty Knightie … um … perhaps not that last one … winner of last year's Golden Lance, Loooorrd Gaunt of Gaunt!' Mad applause erupted around the stadium, and at least three beautiful young ladies in the stands fainted and couldn't be revived until handsome young men were found.

'Aaaaand in the blue corner, in err rusty, hhm, perhaps period armour – *tres ironique* – with just a hint of mud … Siiirrrr Godfrey – *Semper Pronto* – Larkspur.' This less than favourable introduction prompted a smattering of polite applause and more than a few snickers. Someone made a very rude noise.

"Ee's gonner be pulverised!' remarked another audience member, with what might be considered unnecessary relish. At this point, several nervous old ladies had to be led away.

'That poor man, I can't bear to stay!' one was clearly heard to say by Sir Godfrey. Suddenly, his armour felt very hot and heavy.

'Gentlemen! Take your positions!' A striking girl wearing a blue dress and a haughty expression stood up in the Royal Box. She raised a delicate hand and released the small hanky she was holding between finger and thumb. As the scrap of white silk floated to the turf, Gaunt's horse gave a final tremendous snort and thundered towards Sir Godfrey.

At that precise moment a bee decided to sting Clover on

the rump, and Sir Godfrey's afternoon took a turn.

With a lurch, Clover whinnied and broke into a gallop. It was as if Clover, who had spent most of her life in a neat paddock surrounded by gentle lambs, and had not so much as trotted for years, suddenly remembered her generations of breeding as a warhorse. Something stirred deep within; her pupils widened and her nostrils flared. Within seconds both horses had reached their full, thundering speed and the gap between them was closing fast.

Sir Godfrey, who had closed his eyes to begin with, after deciding he'd rather not witness his own death, felt the change in Clover's pace and risked a peek. His mare was moving with grace and a turn of speed he'd never thought possible. Oh my, he thought, this is actually quite fun. Then, when he looked at Gaunt, he couldn't quite believe what he saw. His opponent was racing towards him, but his shield flapped loosely at his side and his lance wasn't quite straight. Ye gods, thought the elderly knight – feeling the green shoots of hope sprout – old Gaunt's underestimating me, he's hardly protecting himself. I might just survive this after all!

Meanwhile, the spectators, sensing something was up, had stopped gossiping and stuffing their faces – so early on in a tournament, it was rare to have two knights go so fast and furious at one another. Perhaps Clover sensed something in the occasion, too, for she found even more pace as the two knights met with

a resounding crash. Sir Godfrey just had time to see Gaunt straighten his lance before he felt his own hit something very big and very hard. He heard it splinter as his whole arm went numb with the force of the impact and he felt the wind being knocked out of him.

The crowd gasped, then roared.

Then, everything went black.

Time passed, the world continued revolving but, for the time being at least, this was of no concern to Sir Godfrey.

The next thing he knew, he was waking up slowly in a white room whose walls seemed to move. There was grass on the floor. He tried to focus and was rewarded with some clarity. That's it; he was in the medical tent. Sir Godfrey turned his head painfully from the floor and looked up. His vision was still a bit blurry, but he could make out his friends Frobisher and Percival, who were peering curiously over him as an old nurse tried to shoo them away.

'He's coming around, ha!' Percival exclaimed.

'Not surprised,' grunted Frobisher. 'You breathing onion and garlic all over him like that would be enough to wake my great-grandfather, and he's been stone dead the last seventy years.' Still half unconscious, Sir Godfrey turned his head the other way and saw a large figure in gunmetal grey, his armour badly crumpled and dented.

The large knight's hand was flapping feebly in the air as he tried to push himself up on his elbows. Funny, Godfrey thought woozily to himself, he looks familiar. Percival's round face poked into view again.

'Knocked him out cold, you did, old chap! Never seen anything like it. Capital lance work ... it was officially called a draw, but you're the toast of the tournament! No-one's unseated Gaunt in five years! He'll be furious when he wakes up ... you knocked him out of the joust!'

'Wha-?'

'Shh, you must rest now, Sir,' the nurse bustled back into view, 'you've got a bad bump on yer noggin. I'll have to ask you two gentlemen to leave.'

'Of course, dear lady.' Percival bowed at the nurse, who pursed her lips as he gave Godfrey a thumbs-up sign behind her back.

'Yes, well done, I suppose, Larkspur.' Frobisher nodded as he retreated towards the medical tent entrance.

His friends gone, Sir Godfrey lay back on his bed. Slowly, deliciously, it all came back to him, as he remembered who the grey knight beside him was and what had happened. Toast of the tournament, he thought to himself, and he smiled hugely before drifting off again.

CHAPTER 8

~: *Joust* :~
· *Part Four. Finale* ·

SIR GODFREY SOON FELT much better and got up, which was just as well, since Lord Gaunt was beginning to stir and he wanted to put off meeting him for as long as possible. A decade or so would do nicely.

He was walking down the main thoroughfare between the stalls that were now beginning to pack up and was looking for his friends when he found, nailed to an oak, the Court's roll of new knights in the kingdom and their maxims – lines that they chose to best describe their noble characters. There were quite a lot, judging by the length of the parchment, and Godfrey felt somewhat sad, and not for the first time, that he and Lady Larkspur had never been able to have children – young squires whose names would one day be added to the list of England's knights.

- Sir Thorganby Ouse; *Defender of the weak*
- The Most Noble Lord Wroot; *Of noble spirit*
- Viscount Dobcross; *Valiant yet humble*
- Sir Flasby Ogden; *Upholder of justice*
- Baron Crumpsall; *Of great mercy*
- Irwene Giddy-Slepe; *Nincompoop*
- Sir Steeple Warmwell; *Mighty sword arm*
- Lord Piddlehinton-Marsh; *Chaste and virtuous*

'Ah there you are! I was just saying to Frobisher here, we'd better get a wiggle on, beat the traffic before it beats us, ha! Feeling better?'

'Um,' Sir Godfrey was still looking at the Giddy-Slepe

entry. 'Yes, I suppose I am.'

'I have it on good authority that you'll get a special mention in the Court circular this year – wouldn't be surprised if you get asked for an audience with his most Royal Majesty Himself!'

'How awful,' opined Frobisher. 'I went to school with him – absolute tick.'

'Yes, well …' said Sir Percival, looking very uncomfortable. For all his joking he was a staunch royalist if ever there was one. 'Here are our lads with the horses and things!' he said.

CHAPTER 9
~: *Bane* :~

BACK AT FOUR FROGS, the summer had just got several times more interesting. The next four days were the best the boys could remember.

Suddenly, the endless days had come alive for them; they would wake at dawn each morning, clamber out of their straw beds and meet by the duck pond in the village square. Then, silently, they would sneak their way through the dew-laden grass and ferns to the woods. At this point, Venn would look carefully around for any early risers on their way to market or out hunting hare, before pulling aside the woven mat of branches that covered the entrance to the secret path that led to the Castle.

Once on the path, the boys would pick up their pace, so that by the time they got to the curtain wall hung with its creepers, through the entrance hall, down the empty corridors and up the Harp Stairs, they were out of breath.

Once inside Rainbeard's study, they would set to work cleaning the Iron Knights; scrubbing the rust off the internal workings and polishing the armour until each one gleamed like highly-polished marble, reflecting the rest of the room in their black, burnished curves and obsidian angles.

Considering that the knights had been neglected for a number of years, Pail was surprised that they were still in relatively good nick. The boys, especially Pail, were intrigued by the strange wires that ran up and down the length of their hollow metal bodies – almost like veins, he thought to himself. Each joint, at the elbow, or knee, for example, was made up of a perfectly fashioned silver ball, resting in a silver cup of the same size, again perfectly imitating what Pail knew to be the joints of a lamb or pig and – he supposed – a human. Equally cool, too, was Bane's sword, which was still as sharp as a brand-new butcher's knife. Venn, who was the only one of them strong enough to lift it with both hands, tried raising it above his head, but just before he reached the apex of an imaginary swing, he dropped it by mistake onto the stone flags. There was a loud clang that seemed to echo around the entire Castle and a fan of sparks that made the boys jump backwards. The vibrations on the floor must have upset a precarious stack of Rainbeard's bottles and jars that had been gathering dust on some shelves nearby because they all fell off at once, resulting in another loud crash the boys were sure could be heard from the village and a series of minor explosions as the spilled contents reacted with each other and promptly blew up.

All three boys looked silently at the deep gouge the sword had made in the solid granite and the bubbling mess of gunk and broken bottles that covered a good portion of the floor space. Then they inspected the shining black surface of the sword, whose blade seemed in no way damaged. 'I know, let's put it back and not touch it ever again,' Giff suggested.

By the end of the second day, their parents – Giff's mum in particular, who knew her son all too well and therefore always feared the worst – were deeply suspicious that their boys left early and did not return until it was nearly dark. And suddenly they were eating almost as much as their fathers. But the three friends had a cover story – they let slip that they had built a tree house in the woods and it was in a secret location so the other children in the village couldn't find it and knock it down. And the parents would smile and sigh – boys would be boys.

Hmm.

It was early afternoon on the fourth day since they had discovered the Iron Knights, and all three were in Rainbeard's study: Giff was fiddling with the brass spying tube, supposedly keeping lookout but actually just making up a running commentary about what was going on in the village. 'Your dad's just fallen in the pond again, Pail. I swear he was ten feet away last time I looked!' Pail didn't comment and tried his best not to look embarrassed. His dad was probably the clumsiest person in the whole county. As a young man, the story went, he'd grown a beard as soon as he could, because shaving could easily mean losing an ear.

Venn was walking around tapping jars of murky liquid and picking things up absentmindedly. Pail was studying the inside of Bane. Now that the Knights were clean, he had hoped he could puzzle out how to get them to work, but so far he hadn't had any luck. All the wires and pulleys inside seemed to move freely but, try as he might, he still couldn't get their arms or legs to budge an inch.

Venn, Pail and Giff had already grown used to being in the Castle and had even begun to feel a little like it was theirs. Going home every evening made the cottages they lived in with their parents and siblings seem almost impossibly small and stuffy in the summer evening heat. Pail fell into musing out loud.

'You know what, apart from that odd mirror downstairs, I haven't actually seen anything magic in this place. Everything else is just sort of inventive – all these cogs and wheels and pulleys. I'm beginning to wonder if Rainbeard was just some kind of clever blacksmith.'

'Well, then how come we can't get these things to work?'

'I guess we just haven't found the walk about lever yet?' replied Pail, still digging about inside Bane. 'Ouch!'

'What's up?' asked Venn, sidling over.

'Oh, nothing, just snagged my finger on one of Bane's

levers. I'm trying to work out these large cogs in his chest – I've got a feeling that they're the key.' He sucked noisily at the bleeding digit before sticking his hand back inside the chest cavity, where the crystal heart was housed in its golden cage. As he did so, a drop of blood fell on the gemstone.

Instantly, the Knight raised an arm, like it was trying to attract the attention of a passing bird.

'Woaaw!' Giff dived under the table and Pail jumped backwards, half falling over a chair.

'Steady, guys,' said Venn, coming forward; before he got any nearer, with another heavy metallic crunching, Bane closed the enormous fist of his raised arm and brought it down on the heavy table. There was a loud crushing noise as the massive lump of solid oak splintered to nothing. Seeing that, even Venn stopped in his tracks.

Slowly, deliberately now, the Knight turned its dark helmet to face the boys. Two pinpricks of angry red light glared through the narrow diagonal slit in the visor. Bane raised his sword arm and Pail could clearly hear the grating of the long-disused gears and levers inside; gears he'd worked very hard cleaning and made sure worked perfectly. Even in his panic, the irony of this wasn't lost on him. Bane pointed the gleaming tip of his sword at Pail and uttered a sort of hollow rasp, somewhere between a hiss and a mechanical growl.

Pail, who up until now had been rooted to the spot, bolted. Giff, who was producing a long-drawn *yaaaaaaahhh* noise, was close behind. Venn, having the presence of mind to slam the heavy door shut behind them, followed in haste.

***

Bane stepped forward with the grace of a dancer and tested the door handle: it moved freely. Then he turned and looked at his two companions. The boy's blood had been good, and it certainly felt better than anything the cruel human who lived here before had ever allowed him. But his master and tormentor had been gone a long time now, and Bane knew something about the frailty of living creatures *of flesh* to feel confident that he was unlikely ever to return.

He paused a while, to savour the magnificent strength that coursed through his insides, pulling taught the thick wires that ran through his body like tendons. He tested his well-oiled joints, coldly pleased at how his limbs moved soundlessly. The others would need blood too, but nothing so exalted as human. Bane moved with graceful menace towards the window where a turtle dove had nested all summer. She had long become used to the shape of the Iron Knight at the window and so suspected nothing until a cold hand shot out with blinding speed. And squeezed hard.

CHAPTER 10
~: Work, Power, Service ~

PAIL AWOKE TO YET ANOTHER fine day. Copper-coloured light from the early morning sun pricked holes in the sparse thatch that covered the cottage he shared with his elderly parents. His brothers and sisters had all left home now and most (eight of them to be exact) were married. So the cottage was still and quiet; the rest of the village of Four Frogs had evidently not got up yet either.

Pail lay still for some time, luxuriating in the thick straw mattress and his soft woollen blanket. He was never going back to the Castle again. That much they were all agreed upon – even Venn. So he felt relaxed and safe, and overnight he had quite convinced himself that what had happened at the Castle yesterday would have nothing to do with anything in the rest of his life.

He was completely wrong in that assumption.

Wrong,
    wrong,
        wrong.

Pail must have drifted off to sleep again, because he didn't notice the shadow of a dark cloud drift across the face of the sun, nor the chill wet wind that seemed to spring up from nowhere.

Time passed. He was eventually woken – as was the rest of Four Frogs – by the sound of incessant bleating and baa'ing and the clatter of cloven hooves on stony ground. It was drizzling quite hard now, and when Pail looked out of the window what he saw was absolute mayhem. Someone had let the sheep out of the enclosure and, just for good measure, had let all the goats out too – plus Mistress Moon's donkey by the looks of it.

The result was that the entire main square was covered with the jostling bodies of livestock running in every direction, knocking things over and churning up the ground into a sodden mass of mud, straw and poo. The other villagers, in various states of undress, were emerging out of their houses into the cold rain, rubbing their eyes and swearing at the barging sheep pursued by butting goats.

Pail looked down the lane in the direction they had come from and felt his heart drop to the pit of his stomach. Strutting up the road, uttering a series of hideous metallic sheep noises was Squawk – it appeared that he hadn't yet worked out how to bend his knees as he walked, and his pointed helmet was covered in bits of straw. It should have looked comical, but there was something terrifying about him. He also seemed greatly excited by the sheep. 'B A A ' R 'k, B A A ' R 'k!' he imitated their bleats and prodded a couple with his spear for good measure. None of the villagers had seen anything quite like it and they instinctively drew themselves back into the shadows of their doorways at his approach. None, that is, except for Venn and Giff, who appeared at their doorways across the square. They looked as sick as Pail felt. 'B A A ' R 'k, B A A ' R 'k!' grated Squawk, looking slightly insane. What have we done, thought Pail. What have we done? Unfortunately, there was worse to come.

Across the square, Giff had returned to his bedroom and was peering out of his window. He caught Pail's eye and made a *don't say anything* sign with his hands, but Venn seemed to be looking in another direction altogether.

DA'HN, DA'HN. A noise like someone hitting a lump of solid metal against a lump of hollow metal came from further up the hill. One by one, everyone tore their attention away from the mayhem in the square and turned around – everyone except Squawk, that is, who still seemed to be transfixed by the sheep.

The huge form of Bludge appeared.

He was striding down the hill, beating his mace against a large black shield, and the sound seemed to echo all around the valley. Behind him, taller, thinner and definitely more sinister, stalked Bane, sure-footed and grim. In between Bludge striking his shield to get attention, Bane seemed to be saying something over and over. At first, no-one could distinguish the words, but gradually, as he drew nearer, Pail heard him repeating, 'Work, power, service … work, power, service, work …' over and over in a similar yet deeper metallic growl. It sounded like iron cogs being wound backwards against their will and crunching gears. 'Work, power, service … work, power, service … work, power, service … work, power, service …'

Then, completely without warning, Bludge stopped beating his shield with his heavy mace and struck the side of the church porch as he went past. Sparks flew up from the stonework and there was a deafening crash as the entire porch disappeared. One minute it had been there, solid and sturdy for generations, the next it was nothing more than a pile of dust and rubble.

Bludge seemed very pleased with the effect and he drew his arm back to strike the main part of the building. Brother Pike, a gangly young man who was new to the village, rushed forward and grabbed the mace in desperation. It was as if he wasn't there and the mace continued to travel through the air, but with Brother Pike attached to it. Luckily, the young monk had enough sense to let go, and he flew sideways as the mace hit its mark against the side of the church. Half of the wall collapsed. At this rate, Bludge was going to destroy the whole building in a matter of minutes.

'stop!' Venn's father, Stirn, stood in the centre of the village square. In one hand he carried a blunt-looking sword, pitted and rusted. It was an old weapon that had belonged to Venn's grandfather, who had once been the village blacksmith. Stirn was the Headman and therefore, by common practice, it was his duty to protect the village. Although he was a large man, built like the blacksmiths his forebears were, he looked puny next to Bludge, who strode forward with a rattling growl.

Venn's father may well have been scared, but he didn't show it. Instead, he stood his ground, waiting until Bludge was within range, then swung the sword in a powerful arc. If Bludge even noticed the attack he didn't show it. The blade hit his coif, the metal plate that ran around his collar like a ruff and would have protected him from having his head chopped off, had there been any head inside the huge iron helm. There was a dull, almost far-away-sounding clang and Stirn's sword snapped in two. Without pause, Bludge carried on moving forward, raised an enormous arm, as thick as the main beam in a house, and slapped the Headman with the back of a mailed fist.

Venn's father may just as well have been hit by a bull. He flipped backwards several feet and crumpled to the ground like a scarecrow without its support. Then Bane stepped forward and pointed his sword at Stirn. 'Work, power, service,' he chanted, kicking a stray piece of stonework towards the villagers who had formed a hesitant semi-circle around the unconscious Stirn. 'Work, power, service!'

'Step back from my father!'

The villagers turned to see Venn standing behind the Iron

Knights, holding the shattered sword in his hand. The rain that was now falling hard had matted his blond hair against his brow and the expression on his face was one of terror, mixed with anger.

The effect on the Iron Knights was electrifying. Even Squawk stopped in his tracks and turned towards Venn, his spear extending in a series of erratic jabbing movements. Bludge uttered a hollow roar and ran at the boy.

It took a heartbeat for everyone to realise that Venn was about to be killed by one of these odd and terrifying creatures. The fastest to react was Giff's dad, who ran forward and grabbed Venn. 'Get off me!' Venn cried, struggling to twist out of Farn's grip on his collar, but Farn held on grimly and dragged Venn into his cottage.

Then a strange thing happened. The moment he disappeared through the doorway, both Bludge and Squawk stopped and went back to what they were doing. Even Bane seemed to shrug, as if he wasn't sure what had just happened, but had forgotten the details anyway. He turned back to Stirn, who was beginning to move weakly.

He pointed his sword at the villagers now, and then at the fallen stone. 'WORK, POWER, SERVICE!' Bane took another step forward – he seemed to be about to thrust the sword into Stirn and no-one could stop him. There was a terrible moment of collective fear amongst the villagers at what might happen.

Just then, Father Mally, the priest, stepped into the circle. He picked up the rock that Bane had kicked. Bane stopped and turned his blank, visored face towards the clergyman. There was total silence, and it seemed to Pail that the moment could go either way. Then, slowly, towering above the priest, Bane pointed a gauntleted finger towards the centre of the square. Father Mally nodded briefly, shuffled over and placed the stone where Bane was pointing,

Chapter 11
~: *Truth* :~

'GOD IS PUNISHING US for our years of sloth. Oh! We basked in the sunlight of apathy, doing nothing all day but stuffing our faces and sleeping whilst our lord and master, the great Rainbeard, was far away, suffering who knows what fate ... oh, shame ... and now these creatures have come to show us the true path and to exact God's revenge. Oh! Woe. The great Knight, our new leader, is right. Work, power, service – it is the only path now! We must follow. We are doomed without it! Doomed, I say!'

'Oh, do please shut up, Terence, especially if you've got nothing sensible to say.' Mistress Smith, Venn's mother, was a formidable woman who wasn't going to let terrible and unexpected events get the better of them.

As Bludge had smashed the church to rubble, the villagers had been prodded by Squawk and terrified by Bane into lifting the heavy stones and making a great pile by the well. No-one was quite sure why they were destroying the beautiful church and what they were supposed to be doing with the rubble, but they quickly found out that if they rested for more than a few moments, Squawk would stop chasing the sheep about and come over and poke them until they got up.

At sundown, the Iron Knights abruptly stopped what they were doing, turned and walked back to the Castle in silence. It was just as well, because the villagers of Four Frogs (and the sheep) could take no more. What Terence had said was partly true: for years they had got by, just growing a few vegetables and keeping the bare minimum of livestock, and the fact was that none of them were used to doing any really hard work.

It had rained all day and now they were huddled in Stirn's cottage – all of them wet, shivering and exhausted – trying to figure out what had happened and what they were going to do about it.

'Perhaps Terence is right, perhaps we are being punished?' said Mistress Pittle, who lived near the wood and was apt to think gloomy thoughts.

'Nonsense,' replied Venn's mum, 'they're not God's creatures – they're man made and can be broken by man too. We just need to stand up to them!'

'Stand up to them, Maisy? You saw what happened to your husband … and it was going to kill your son,' Giff's mum – her sister – said as forcefully as she dared.

'Then we'll just have to find Rainbeard and ask him to come back,' shouted someone at the back, lost in the dense fog of smoke from the fire in the middle of the room.

At this, Stirn, the Headman, stirred himself. He still looked pale but otherwise seemed in one piece after his brief, one-sided fight with Bludge. 'We don't know where he's gone, no-one's heard from him for almost a generation.' He paused as he looked around the room, staring at each person in turn, as if to re-stamp his authority on the villagers individually, an authority that had been badly dented. But even injured, he was still a force to be reckoned with. Most people were unable to meet his hard gaze for long, dropping their own eyes after a few heartbeats. Satisfied for now, Stirn cleared his throat. 'And who says it's anything to do with him or even something he can do anything about?'

'They came from the direction of the Castle,' Farn pointed out, not unreasonably.

'They could have just arrived – using it 'cos they found it's empty,' said someone else.

Farn shook his head. 'There's weird things up there; new-fangled, magic things we don't understand. Dangerous stuff.'

'And how do you know, have you ever been up there?' Stirn stared at his brother-in-law.

'No, er … I –'

But before Farn could go on, a voice that sounded like wind blowing down a cracked chimney wheezed into life. It was Granny Avfeldig – the oldest person in the village. 'Oh, they come from the Castle, alright. I 'erd tell rumours of 'em when I was a little girl. Evil things, mistakes, wizardy meddling gone wrong that the old man kept locked away to protect us and everybody else!' Up until then, the room had been subdued but with the usual shuffling and coughing as a background noise that you always get at gathering. Now there was a new kind of silence, the sort that spelled avid attention. You could hear a fly chewing. Granny shook her head. 'No, them's been woken by someone. Someone who's been up at the old Castle … you mark my words! And we'll all suffer for it!'

The room erupted. Indignant cries of 'No!' and 'Of course not!', 'It's too well guarded,' and 'No-one would be that stupid,' rang out in the now stuffy room that had just got a lot hotter for Venn, Giff and Pail.

This was Pail's moment.

Racked with guilt all day, he had tried to help with the rocks, but the effect of Giff, Venn or Pail on the Knights was the same each time. The instant any of them were spotted, all three Knights would stop what they were doing and charge the boys, uttering clanking cries of hatred. Luckily, the villagers had assumed it was something the Iron Knights had against children in general and so anyone under fifteen was kept inside all day, out of harm's way.

But Pail had to tell the truth now, and so he opened his mouth to speak.

At that very moment, someone shouted across him, cutting through the noise in the room.

'It was me!' shouted Giff, 'I did it … it's all my fault!' Each and every person in the room stopped and stared at him through the smoke.

'What do you mean?' asked Stirn.

'I …' Giff paused. Being brave was harder than he had imagined, and suddenly his mouth felt like it was full of cold ash, but he swallowed hard, and took a deep breath. 'I went to the Castle … er, on my own, I was messing around, and I woke up the Knights … by accident.'

'He's lying!' Venn stepped forward. He placed himself in front of his father. It was funny; Pail had never noticed just how similar they were before. 'I was there too, it's probably more my fault, I persuaded him to go in.'

All this was more than Pail could take. 'That's not right! It was my blood that spilled, I woke them … or at least one of them … Bane – he's the biggest one with the sword – he must have woken the others, that's Squawk and Bludge … when we ran away.'

Dead, dumbfounded silence.

The tension built, Pail feeling like he was standing in a deep well looking up at the adults, then the room erupted in fury. Angry shouts flew around; Pail felt himself being jostled and he even saw Giff knocked to the ground by an angry slap.

'SILENCE!' roared Stirn. 'THIS IS MY HOUSE, I AM THE HEADMAN AND YOU WILL HEAR ME BEFORE ANY ONE OF YOU LAYS ANOTHER FINGER ON THESE BOYS! OR … OR, YOU WILL HAVE ME TO ANSWER TO!' Stirn stood up for the first time, his broad shoulders filling the space between the fire and the seated villagers who instinctively drew back. Stirn glared about the room again as if daring anyone else to speak, then he turned to Pail who felt himself shrivel up under his gaze. '*You*. Ran. Away?' he reiterated, slowly and very deliberately. There was incredulity and menace in his tone. Venn stepped forward, between Stirn and Pail.

'We *all* did, Father. We went into the Castle, just to get Giff's money bag back. Then we found the Iron Knights and we woke them up by accident. We ran … we were scared …' Stirn tore his eyes from Pail and looked at his son, seemingly for the first time in his life.

'And you didn't tell anyone what you had done?'

Venn bit his lip. 'No, Father. I am sorry.'

Stirn raised his hand, and for an instant it looked like he would strike his own son, but then he caught his wife's eye. She was crying. His hand dropped to his side. With a huge effort, Pail lifted his face and saw his parents. His mother stared at him with a curious intense expression he couldn't quite fathom, but his father just turned his face away, as if he couldn't bear to look at his own son. Pail knew what he had to do.

'We'll go to the Castle. You've seen them; it's us they want. We did this, we'll sacrifice ourselves.'

Giff and Venn nodded and a lot of the other villagers seemed to like the idea.

'Hear, hear.'

'First good idea someone's had all evening.'

'Let's send 'em up there right now!'

' – no sense in hanging about.'

Stirn shook his head. 'No-one is going near the Castle and no-one is going to look for Rainbeard. This is our problem and we'll sort it out on our own. As for the boys, these *Iron* Knights seem to have something against them. For their own good, they must be sent away!'

'You can't turn them away, they're children!' Venn's mother cried out, but her husband's face was set.

'It's for their safety, Maisy … it's not a punishment.' Even for a strong man with his authority now renewed, he still couldn't quite look at her.

'But …' Pail's mother, who had never said a word at a village meeting in her whole life, ran towards her son. 'He's just a boy … he didn't understand!'

'It's not a punishment,' repeated Stirn, 'if we take them to the Chalk Road tomorrow, before daybreak, we'll ask the first tinkers or travellers to take them. They're strong lads and healthy. They can work. Any traveller would be glad to have them.' He looked once more around the room. 'So it's settled.'

People nodded. He still had enough authority to proclaim his decision without anyone daring to openly disagree, and with that the meeting broke up. There were still a few grumbles but everyone was exhausted and just wanted to rest. No-one was in any doubt that tomorrow would be the same and, in any case, the culprits were just children and being sent away was punishment enough.

For now they just wanted their beds.

CHAPTER 12

~: *Leaving* :~

FROBISHER WAS DOING what Frobisher was best at. He was grumbling.

Chilly rain had poured down since they left the tournament and everything they had was soaking wet, including their spare clothes and food. He took a bite of soggy bread and a nibble of damp sausage and washed it down with some very watery beer.

'This is the worst breakfast I've had since the cook went down with cauldron elbow and we all had to take it in turns. Chaffinch, my head librarian, and Stregthorn, the Master-at-Arms, both had a bash at it. They had an argument over creative control and we all assumed that Chaffinch ended up in the stew. Lucy, the stable girl, swore she found a big toe in her portion, and had to go and lie down. Chaffinch *did* actually turn up about a week later, but not until Cook came back and found him upside down in the compost. Poor man's never been quite the same since.'

'What's that up ahead?' Sir Godfrey wasn't really listening and Percival was still asleep in the back of the cart, which carried all their armour as well as Percival's "absolutely bloody essential" barrels of wine.

Frobisher spent too much time reading in poor candlelight and his eyesight was poor. 'Not sure,' he said, 'this isn't a travel game is it? I really hate travel games.'

'No,' Godfrey peered through the sheets of rain, 'it looks like someone's trying to attract our attention.'

'Then we'll do our best to ignore them.'

By and by, they drew level with the small group. A burly man – a peasant, judging by his dress, but with a natural air of authority – had his arm raised, partly in greeting and partly to call them over. Sir Godfrey turned soggily in his saddle with a squelch.

'Yes, how can we be of assistance?' he asked, noticing that the man's companions were in fact just children. Grubby and rather unhappy-looking boys, by the looks of it.

'Begging your pardon, Sir, but we've been waiting here since before dawn. You're the first people to come along this way and, with the weather as it is, I think you'll probably be the last …'

'Tell him to get on with it,' interrupted Frobisher. 'When we stop the rain starts to trickle down the back of my trousers.'

'It's like that song everyone was singing in the taverns last year – *I'm just chillin' with my Britches*.' Percival had woken up. 'What's going on now?'

'I don't know.' Although it was pouring, Sir Godfrey noticed the strain around the peasant's eyes. 'What is it, man? What do you want of us?' The peasant seemed taken aback to be talking to what was quite obviously a nobleman. This road is probably only used by merchants and travelling folk, thought Godfrey. We only went this way because Frobisher was sure it was a shortcut.

'I want … I mean, my Lord, I do humbly beg you to take these boys.'

'Take 'em? Take 'em where? We've no room and really no time to give grubby little boys lifts places!'

The man seemed to sag. 'This is not going as I planned,' he muttered to himself. 'My Lord,' he said, 'it is for their own safety, they *must* get away from here … our village, that is … they're good boys … well,' he paused, 'they're boys … but they're stout-hearted, they don't eat much and they'll work well. This one's clever too … he can read!'

Godfrey looked at the boys again and noticed something

else, something very important. 'But this one is your own son,' he said gently, pointing to the biggest boy who was doing his best to look brave.

For a moment, the man standing on the side of the road, trying to give up his own son to strangers, looked like he couldn't trust himself to speak. 'Yes,' he replied huskily, 'yes he is, but ...' he faltered as his voice cracked; he took a deep breath and mastered himself again. 'You must see, then, that they have to go away. And I wouldn't do it unless I had to, my wife's heart is broken, I've never seen her like this.'

Sir Godfrey perceived for the first time, but not the last, that having children opened your heart to the greatest love and also the deepest despair. The rain seemed to ease off around their small gathering, like a tunnel of stillness. He and the man looked at one another for a long time.

'You seem a kind man ... Sire.'

'I can take one,' said Sir Godfrey, making the first snap decision of his entire life. 'I will take your son and I will look after him well, I give you my word. He seems a fine boy!'

'And I will take the other, this chap here – seems to me he's got a twinkle in his eye.' Percival had climbed down from the cart and was standing in the rain, looking unusually grave for once. He bowed. 'Again, I give you my word as a knight of this realm that he'll be cared for.'

Stirn watched as both gentlemen turned and looked at Frobisher, who was glaring at the back of his horse's head. To anyone else, he would have appeared the very picture of disinterest; his friends, who had known him since he was a boy, could see he was deeply moved. Eventually, he looked up. 'The skinny one can read, you say?'

The Big Booke of
Knightes &
Chivalrie

What each & everie Squire needeth knowe
to become a Goode Knighte
(but was afeared to ask)

Copied out from the original by Illuminated Guides C M L X V I I
*The vellum used in this publication was 100% recycled from
a S H E E P E naymed Fluffie*

Equipment

The modern knighte, to be taken seriously, requires certain basic items that need to be purchased (if not already inherited or taken from a Vanquished Foe). The list below is a guide and does not include accessories that may seem essential, like: a good-sized castle, Faire Maide, small Home County.

1. Steeds:
⚜ Good horse &
spare horse ·

2. Weapons:
⚜ Broadsword ·
⚜ Bastard Sword ·

⚜ Falchion ·
⚜ Greatsword ·
⚜ Lances x 3 ·
⚜ Spear ·
⚜ Mace ·
⚜ Morning star ·

It went on...

3. Armour:

- On Hedde ·
- Close helm ·
- Great helm ·
- Frog mouth ·
- Hounskull ·
- Lobster tail pot ·
- Mail coif ·
- Nasal helmet ·
- Sallet ·
- Spangenhelm ·
- Kettle hat ·
- Visor ·
- Falling buffe ·
- Nossel ·

On...

Neck
- Aventail ·
- Bevor ·
- Gorget ·
- Pixane ·

Chest
- Brigandine ·

- Cuirass ·
- Culet ·
- Plackart ·
- Fauld ·
- Hauberk ·
- Codpiece ·
- Lance rest ·
- Loin-guard ·

And on...

Arms & handes
- Ailette ·
- Besagew ·
- Couter ·
- Gauntlet ·
- Pauldron ·
- Rerebrace ·
- Spaulder ·
- Vambrace ·

Leg x 2
- Chausses ·
- Cuisses ·
- Greave ·
- Poleyn ·
- Sabaton ·
- Schynbald ·
- Tasset ·

WARNING

ON NO ACCOUNT MUST THE KNIGHTE ATTEMPT
TO WEAR ALL ITEMS AT ONCE, ESPECIALLY IF BATHING!

4. Sundries:
- Shield ·
- Lute ·

5. Clothes
- Vest ·

- Jumper ·
- Goode trousers ·
- Badde trousers ·
- Socks ·
- Cleane Hankie ·

Upkeepe

A knighte must bathe at least once a month in running water (stream, river), not a well, which is considered simply poore manners.

He must also shave – no long hair, or dirty nails – like catte.

Daily life

Drunkenness: no knighte should drink meade, beere, apple cider before dawn or to excess. No more than 15 pints of each should be consumed a day, particularly with strong drinkes such as fortified wine, unless questing. A Gentil knighte should not be drunk if jousting.

Good knighte's sleep. At dusk prayers, then up at dawn, prayers. Lunch, more prayers.

Physical prowess

You must be afraid of nothing but God and dishonour.
A knighte also must:
- Be able to endure extreme hardship e.g. grate heat, cold, storms, and badde food.
- Be able to perform a somersault from standing, whilst wearing his helmet. Or backwards from his horse.
- Slice apple in three equal parts with a broadsword.
- Walk along a rope blindfolded.
- Looke goode in tights.

Learning

A knighte must:

- Speak Latin, Greek and French and read with a fine sonorous voice.
- Dance an estampie or rondeau.
- Play lute or viele.
- Recite chansons and lais most merrily.

BUT to whosoever wishes to become a goodly knighte and win the respect and love of his fellowe knightes-in-arms, all these things mean no more than the proud crow of the foolish cockerill who struts and preens and imagines himself the fiercest most handsome creature in the castle (and not the most ridiculous).

SO, it is most essential that every knighte in the Kingdom have:

Honour

A knighte who encounters a rascal, knave or knowne foe must challenge with cries of "Jackanape!" or risk dishonour – a fate worse than death.

Once joined in battle the knighte must use all force to vanquish his foe but must never be tempted into the use of vile instruments of pain such as the: Iron Maiden (coffin with spikes); Pear of Anguish (screws and things); Brazen Bull (really nasty, doesn't bear thinking about – no really – just take our word for it), Judas Cradle (ditto); Rack (stretching limbs), boiling (self-explanatorie), burning or
RATS.

Friendshippe and Loyaltie

The most noble and honourable of all pursuits is that of friendshippe and loyaltie with his fellowe knightes.

- A true friend is one who is with you when everyone else would rather be somewhere else.
- A loyal friend is someone who believes in you when you have ceased to believe in yourself.

Justice and Mercy

Justice is the reason behind the quality of mercy that the knighte must show all others. For mercy bears fruits far greater than that of stricte justice ...

PAIL LOOKED UP from the slim, silver-bound volume Frobisher had given him. He was in the South Library – one of three in the castle – about half way up one the turrets that looked out over the River Ex as it meandered its way through the Wessex countryside.

The hedgerows were filled with the usual sort of thing that hedgerows made a good home for, and skylarks filled the air with sound and movement as they banked and dived around the towers and high walls.

He had been with Lord Frobisher for nearly seven years now and nothing he had read in all that time had affected him so much nor touched him so deeply as the words he now read. Phrases tumbled in his head – the knight's code of nobility, loyalty, and mercy suddenly made sense to him because it gave life a sort of gentle order and the fairness he craved.

Up until now, he had only vague ideas about true knights. They had seemed as remote to him as characters in a book – they were not real people, only mere ideas, and not very realistic ones at that. Where had the change in heart come from?

The books he'd been reading lately had certainly spurred it on, but the transformation had come about gradually. The more time he spent with Lord Frobisher, in fact.

honos ~ amicitia ~ fides

He wrote at the top of a letter he intended to write. Then he paused; his brown eyes half closed, his thin, pale face thoughtful. He cast his mind back all those years, his thoughts twisting down the tunnels and oubliettes of his memories, rediscovering those strange, early days at Eruditas Castle, the family seat for over three hundred years of his master and friend.

The morning after they had arrived from their muddy journey all those years ago, Frobisher had come down (extremely late) for his breakfast and glared at the younger Pail for quite a long time. Pail, who'd never sat down on a real chair at a real table for his breakfast, still less one that was longer than his entire house, began to feel nervous. Somehow, the feeling was made worse by the fact that Frobisher was a good fifteen yards away.

'Good morning, Sir,' he hazarded eventually.

'Balderdash!' snapped Frobisher and promptly left the room.

The next morning, Pail – who'd spent the rest of the day in his bed chamber, not daring to move – came down for his breakfast and was very relieved to find the dining hall empty, save for a couple of wolfhounds who loped over to sniff his legs and then lick his hand.

After breakfast, he felt a bit more daring and decided to go off and explore on his own. He'd been there a day and yet he'd only seen one other person apart from Frobisher – the squire, Simkin, who always seemed to be out of breath, running around and completing a seemingly limitless list of errands. He didn't seem much inclined to answer any enquiries the boy might have, even if he'd stuck around long enough for Pail to compose a question sufficiently brief. Truth was, Pail had hundreds of questions, but he was bright enough to realise that most answers would come to him in due course – of their own accord, when good and ready.

The answer to his main question – namely, what did everyone actually do in this huge crumbling place that was so unlike Rainbeard's Castle; packed to the rafters as it was with books, furniture, tapestries, rusting armour, chipped statues and vast numbers of sleeping dogs – came to him much sooner than he expected.

He'd been wandering about the corridors for a while when he heard Frobisher shouting at someone from behind a heavy door. 'No, no, you complete ignoramus, what do I even give you house space for! *Herb and Planetary Remedies* is not a Greek tragedy, unless you count one of Cook's cures for coughs and influenza where, I do freely admit, it is more than quite likely that everyone important will be dead before it is time to go home ... and, aaargh! What's this? You've only gone and put *Beowulf* in the Pets section ... Get out, before I have you locked in a gibbet until Michaelmas!'

It had been Pail's intention to sneak by unnoticed at that point, but this plan was scotched when a small man, wearing a huge pair of ivory spectacles, flung the door open. The librarian, Chaffinch (for it was he), looked very close to tears. He rushed past Pail as if he hardly noticed the boy was there and scurried down a flight of steps. Pail, who couldn't resist, peered into the room the small man had just left in such a hurry.

Two large stained glass windows may have made up most of the back wall, but both sides of the chamber comprised of one huge bookshelf reaching from the floor to the ceiling, which was at least sixty foot high. Frobisher was at the top of a truly lethal-looking ladder, which tapered to almost nothing at its end. He was scanning rows of tattered leather-bound volumes whilst uttering some of the worst language that Pail had ever heard (in his relatively short career of learning rude words from Giff). The old knight craned around before Pail could creep off.

'You there, yes, you, skinny boy ... don't look like that, you are skinny ... I'm told you can read, come here please!'

Unbelievably, the rest of the day had been utter bliss. The room housed the second largest library in Eruditas Castle and Frobisher was in the process of cataloguing it.

Even he was pleased with Pail's progress, although he could scarcely bring himself to admit it. 'Yes, well, you're not completely dense and, although clearly bone-idle – or else we would have got through indexing *Viking Bashing People Up Songs* and *Woad, interesting things to do with it at home* – I suppose you're just about better employed here than in the kitchens … come back tomorrow, midday, sharp!'

Chapter 2
~: *Eruditas Castle* :~

APART FROM CHAFFINCH,[2] Eruditas Castle was full of all sorts of people who ran the place like a small town. Eruditas even resembled its owner – being tall, thin and poised as if to topple over at any moment after a strong gust of wind. Rainbeard's Castle, Pail realised, was also a reflection of its master – mysterious and absent – or at least, virtually empty. Absent of life, then – apart from the Iron Knights, if they could be called alive.

The man largely responsible for Chaffinch's nervous disposition – Stregthorn, the Master-at-Arms – basically made sure that the place was well-defended – although from whom or against what Pail was completely mystified. England was going through a rare period of peace and most raiding parties from across the channel or the North Sea were kept at bay by the solid coastal defences. As far as Pail could make out, then, Stregthorn's main duty was bullying people.

Early on in his exile, Pail had experienced this first hand. It had started with small things – an outstretched leg as he walked by, making him trip, followed by a friendly cuff that wasn't that friendly. Pail reacted at first as if he hadn't noticed but he was homesick and he had to admit Stregthorn scared him. 'Do they all walk around like they got their noses stuck in the air round where you come from?' Stregthorn had accosted Pail early one evening on his way to supper. In response, Pail did his best to smile politely and

---

[2] Who quickly and gratefully retired to a quiet corner of one of the smaller libraries, where he was left cataloguing seemingly endless tomes on bumblebees, field mice and earwigges.

sidestep around the much larger man but Stregthorn was quicker and he shouldered Pail roughly who bounced off the wall, cutting the corner of his eye. 'Or is that why they kicked you out, 'cos you think you're better than everyone?' He said as he strolled away, leaving Pail still sitting on the floor, wondering what he had done to upset the Master-at-Arms.

Two weeks later, he had been walking under the Postern's Arch, carrying a pile of papers for Frobisher and doing his best not to drop them in one of the numerous puddles that littered the courtyard. As usual, he was lost in gloomy thoughts about home, missing his parents and feeling guilty over the Iron Knights, when he felt the sudden, marrow-freezing sensation of very cold water tipping over his head and down his back. It was followed, presumably for good measure, by a couple of bullet-hard turnips and an evil-smelling tomato. Pail looked up, expecting a profuse apology from a scullion, but all he got was a rotten cabbage in his face. 'Better watch where yer goin' lad – you get some funny rain in these parts, har, har, har!' Stregthorn held up an empty leather bucket whilst a couple of castle guards doubled up in howls of nasty-sounding laughter.

Pail had managed to get most of the rotten vegetable and water stains off of the manuscripts he'd been carrying but he must have still smelled pretty suspect, because as soon as he came into the South Library, Frobisher had almost fallen off his lectern. 'Ye gods!' he exploded, 'did you sleep in the pigsty or have you eaten something that died last spring?' For Pail, this was almost the last straw. He had never been away from home before, still less knew when he was going back, nor had he any idea what was happening to his family whilst he was gone. He nearly burst into tears on the spot.

'No, I … was walking … archway … must have been … um … just an accident …' he mumbled, his bottom lip quivering. Frobisher, who had a habit of staring, softened his features a fraction.

'Our sort,' he said, after a longish pause, 'the quiet ones, the readers and the scribblers, we've always been what you might call a target for bullies.' Frobisher came down the lectern steps and took the scrolls from the boy's hand, frowning briefly at the few remaining stains. 'Now, young man: I could either get you to name the culprit and punish him, ostensibly for damaging some manuscripts that are probably worth more than five years of his miserable little salary, but that won't help you in the long run. Or, I could simply let slip that his chambers are at the foot of the Beggars Gate and let you fight your own battles.' Frobisher straightened up, his knee joints creaking alarmingly. 'I haven't decided yet, but for now you'd best go and get clean. Go and ask Lucy to boil some water for a bath in the kitchens. And tell her I said you may try some of my own supply of sugared raspberries in brandy – I daresay you'll find they're excellent – as you naturally would expect, seeing 's I made 'em meself!'

Later, luxuriating in his first ever hot bath, eating his first ever Frobisher brandy-drenched raspberry, Pail had an idea.

❧

The next day, Cook was chatting to Lucy in the pantry. 'I saw old Stregthorn today, as I was collecting the eggs. He was acting a bit funny, if you ask me, pushing that helmet of his this way an' that an' mutterin' to hisself. He quite forgot to steal any of the eggs off me or try and break them as he went past. "You alright?" I asks. "No," he replies, "no I ain't!" and he walks off without another word.'

In fact, Stregthorn wasn't himself for a whole week: one day he complained to anyone who would listen that his helmet was too big, and yet the next he would insist that it was far too small and that his head was being squeezed like a ripe plum. He began to take on a haunted expression and was often heard muttering to himself distractedly. People would have felt sorry for him were it not for the fact that a preoccupied Stregthorn meant he left them in peace. No-one got shouted at, or had water thrown at them, or got thrown in piles of dung.

Very early one morning, the unhappy Master-at-Arms was heard all over the castle, shouting at people who were coming into the courtyard to sell their wares at the weekly market. A face appeared high up in the Keep.

'STREGTHORN!' Stregthorn froze. 'Stregthorn, yes, you there man! What in the blazes do you think you are doing yelling at this hour right underneath my window? It's practically still midnight!'

The mere sight of Frobisher in his nightshirt was alarming enough, but Frobisher had the power to make Stregthorn's life a misery and the Master-at-Arms knew it.

'Begging your most 'umble pardon, Sire. I'm out of sorts today. My helmet, it's too tight and it's making my 'ed hurt terrible. Yesterday, it was too loose! One day me head shrinks, the next it's blown up like a balloon. I must be dying or very sick, at least.' Frobisher, who had been about to shout something very rude before going back to bed, paused with the ghost of a smile crossing his thin lips.

'Talk to the young lad, the new tic – Pail's his name!' he advised. His head went in but reappeared almost immediately. 'And I don't want to hear another sound until at least midday from you or anyone else. So you can tell those children over there to keep quiet, and any goats coming over the cobbles will have to tiptoe, or I might just decide to order kid stew tonight. And that goes for the lot of them!'

A little while later, Pail was in his chambers catching up on some light reading, when he heard a tentative knock at the door. He looked at the rivet gun and pliers on his desk and quietly slid them into a drawer. 'Come in!' he said, putting on what he hoped was an innocently enquiring expression. The Master-at-Arms' head appeared around the door. To Pail he looked like a man in great pain and terrible anguish.

'Begging your pardon, er, Master Pail, Lord Frobisher said you'd be the man to talk to.'

'About what?' said Pail now concentrating on his book, 'As you can see, I'm quite busy!'

'Oh, yes! I'm so sorry, of course you are … and I wouldn't presume to disturb you, but I have this problem and it's affecting me something terrible.' Pail's eyes didn't shift from the book as he licked a finger nonchalantly and turned a page.

'What is it?'

'It's me noggin, it's changing size every day – goes big and small like it's got a mind of its own. I can feel me brain turning to mush with all this squeezing and expanding. His Lordship is sure you can help … oh, and I'm ever so sorry about the other day … it was those guards' idea … they can be a bit, er … playful at times, but you can count on me seeing it never 'appens again.'

Pail nodded wisely, doing his utmost not to smile. 'Well, I can certainly see why Lord Frobisher sent you here. Around our parts, I'm sorry to say that this is quite a common problem – unfortunately it is usually fatal, if left untreated!' At this Stregthorn staggered sideways and had to hold on to the wall.

'I knew it! Oh! Master Pail, you've got to 'elp. Is there a cure? Tell me there is … I'll do anything, I'll pay anything.

I don't want to die, I ain't even been to the seaside yet.'

'Yes,' Pail went on, half to himself, 'it's a painful way to go and, rather, er, smelly …'

'Whaaat?' Stregthorn hung on to the stone pillar for dear life.

'… symptoms include cranial expansion and shrinkage, oafish behaviour and a stupid expression – rather like that of a particularly dim goose.' Pail stopped, concerned that he may have gone too far. He needn't have worried though.

'That's me in a nutshell!' exclaimed Stregthorn. 'Ooh, yer brainy! But what can I do?' Pail finally looked up, meeting the large man's gaze levelly. Stregthorn, when not kicking people about the castle, could usually be found stuffing his chops in the kitchens. As a result, he was getting quite fat. Pail allowed a silence to develop that became uncomfortable. Stregthorn squirmed.

'It's a long shot,' said Pail, eventually, 'but first and foremost, try a diet of cold vegetables, dry bread and water. Secondly, lots of quiet; no excitement, sudden movements and definitely no shouting …'

There was lots of vigorous nodding. 'Yes, yes, I can do that.'

Pail held up a long finger for silence. '… but most important of all, you must do at least one good deed a day. It will invigorate the blood and, er … it will reduce brain fluctuations by altruistic, holistical increments. You have a sixty percent chance of making a full recovery within ten years … provided that you keep this up.'

Stregthorn looked like he would weep with gratitude. 'Oh, Master Pail, how can I ever thank you enough?'

'Don't mention it, Stregthorn,' Pail replied casually, wondering why he had ever been afraid of the Master-at-Arms, 'your good health is reward enough for me.'

'Ooh, you're a saint!'

'I suppose I am … but keep it under your hat.'

Pail watched the door close. Once he was sure Stregthorn was halfway down the corridor, he opened his drawer and looked at the hidden tools. One more visit tonight to put the helmet back to its usual size and he wouldn't be needing these again. Pail permitted himself a broad smile. He had learned two important things that day: first of all, solving problems yourself was immensely rewarding and secondly, a bit of brainpower and planning can go a long way.

Applying his undoubted cleverness and a bit of charm along the way, Pail was very soon as much a useful part of Eruditas Castle as anyone there. With the virtual retirement of Chaffinch, Pail became Lord Frobisher's closest assistant – helping out not just with the library but in the Assizes (the court that Frobisher as Lord presided over, dealing with local disputes and criminal proceedings) and the daily running of Eruditas, which soon became a bustling hive of activity and a haven for artists, painters and writers from all over the kingdom.

The years passed.

One evening, Pail was in the long hall where he had sat alone with his breakfast all those years before, just a frightened boy. Autumn was well on its way and a fire was blazing in the huge hearth. Pail, full of roast boar and bread soaked in dripping, felt his eyelids begin to droop.

'Ahem!'

Pail sat up straight. 'My Lord!' he said, trying but failing to stifle a yawn.

'Pail,' intoned Frobisher as he sat down heavily in a deep leather seat opposite the young lad. Normally that would have been it – both of them sitting in companionable silence, reading until it was time to go to bed. That evening, though, something seemed to be bothering Frobisher – he fidgeted in his seat, then fiddled with the book he was meant to be reading. He kept looking up at Pail, opening his mouth as if to say something, then closing it again.

Eventually Pail began to lose patience. 'Sir?'

In response, Frobisher shot him a hunted look, but did his best to adopt a conversational tone. 'I have no doubt that in the coming generations books will be read the world over – everyone will have at least a dozen, I dare say. This is a sort of dream of mine. But books aren't everything. Sometimes, well … a book can simply be the start of something.' He turned an expensive, silver-clasped volume over in his hands – it was a book that Pail had never seen before.

'Er, yes, Sir.'

'Anyway, humprh … as you know … you've been here a while now and, um,' at that point Frobisher seemed to have a coughing fit.

'Shall I get you some brandy, Sir?'

'Yes, er, no, stay where you are, sit.' Frobisher waggled a finger, 'sit, sit … yes, well, where was I? Ah, yes … you came to Eruditas, all those years ago, wet behind the ears … but you've come on, and I've come to appreciate you, rely on you even … I've had no children of my own, as you know … but if I had a son…' Frobisher looked like he was about to die of embarrassment at this point in the conversation, but he struggled on bravely: '… then I'd be proud if he was like you. I just hope you have been happy here?'

'Yes, Sir, yes I have …' said Pail with feeling.

'But, I am not your father,' interrupted the old Lord, 'and you must be missing your mother, your brothers and sisters.' It was the first time in seven years Frobisher had ever mentioned them – Pail was momentarily speechless, which was just as well, as Frobisher was still struggling to get something off his chest. 'Now, I don't know why you had to leave the village, but I have developed the strong impression over the years that there is some unfinished business back home.' Pail nodded. 'Quite, so I thought, and what I, er ... what I wanted to say was that, whilst I value you here, you have now reached an age where doing something is sometimes more important than simply ... um, er ... oh, I don't know, damn and blast! I've never been any good at this sort of thing. What I am trying to say, I suppose, is that you should read this. I think it will help!' And with that, Lord Frobisher thrust the leather-bound book into the boy's hands and left the room.

Pail turned the cover over in his hands:

Knightes and Chivalrie
It said.

And so that was how he came to be reading books about knights, and wishing, for one reason alone, but with all his heart that he was one.

⚜

In spite of the early autumn sunlight, Pail shivered. Reading about knights had turned his thoughts to the iron-clad monstrosities that they had woken up all those years ago. It goes without saying that since then, Pail, when not working for his master, had applied his considerable brain to working out strategies to get rid of them.

The guilt he felt at what they had done had only got worse with each passing season. It followed him about the castle like his own shadow; happy though he was most of the time, he was never truly at peace. However, until now,

PART III
Return

CHAPTER I
~: *Gathering* :~

Frost hung in the air, catching the horse's breath, transforming it into twin plumes of smoke as it snorted and pawed the ground impatiently.

This was a warhorse – a great, sleek beast – all sinews, shining armour and taught muscle. Havoc was bred for one reason only – charging enemy lines thick with spears, through squalls of arrows, amidst the clash of steel, blade and bone. And loving it.

So basically, hanging about on freezing hillsides at dawn for no apparent reason was not his idea of a fitting warhorse pastime.

His rider, dressed in a mail shirt and leather trewes, extended a gloved hand and patted the horse's neck, calming it in an instant. If Venn felt the cold, he hardly showed it. Years in Sir Godfrey's household had toughened and changed him almost beyond recognition.

Feeling almost entirely responsible for what had happened at Rainbeard's Castle, he had started his stay at Beaufoy Castle as a strict penance. Refusing chambers in the castle itself, he had insisted on sleeping with the oxen in the winter, in their battered, damp shed. When the weather got warmer, he would move outside the castle, spending his nights camping in the dense woods that surrounded the few farms the Godfreys still owned.

Every morning, at dawn, he would present himself at the stables or the blacksmiths and he would work until nightfall, long after all the other servants had gone home. Then, he would trudge over to the window of the kitchens and accept whatever they had for him with a solemn look and murmured thanks.

The cook, who had eight children of her own and twice as many grandsons and daughters, would pretend to scold him every evening about not looking after himself and Venn would pause, nod and thank her again for the food and her kindness. In her heart though, she felt like taking him straight home and mothering him. Lady Godfrey Larkspur, who would talk to Venn when she went for her daily walk, was similarly moved to pity in those first few years, especially each time she saw the chilblains and weeping calluses on his hands.

Then she would go and see her husband and entreat him to make Venn come in to the castle, even for just a few nights. 'You promised his father, did you not, that you would look after him as if he were your own?'

'Yes, dear.' Sir Godfrey would say. 'But what can I do, if he refuses any comforts? I can hardly clap him in irons, drag the poor boy inside and lock him up.'

Lady Godfrey would shake her head. 'Would you let your own son freeze with the cattle in the winter, work harder than the lowest prisoner, share his bed with the wolves and brigands in the forest?' and Sir Godfrey would sigh.

'No your Ladyship, I would not, but the boy thinks he has done something, it has altered him – he seems ashamed of this thing and I feel that kindness will somehow make it worse … you must let him work it out in his own way.'

But Elspeth Godfrey had firm opinions on this particular subject. 'Children are incapable of real wickedness. If they do a wrong thing, however bad, it is almost always the fault of an adult, somewhere along the line.'

For his part, Sir Godfrey found Venn a thoroughly likeable boy who, when not working, was full of intelligent questions – mainly about the horses and the smithy. After a few months, Sir Godfrey persuaded Grigg, the castle blacksmith, to take him on as an apprentice. Grigg, who had seven daughters and liked a bit of peace and quiet at work, took to Venn almost immediately. 'The boy's a natural,' he told his master, 'already strong as a bullock and – best of all, Sire – no chit chat.'

As soon as Venn had mastered the rudiments of beating metal, he set about making a sword.

In seven whole years, he had never once set foot inside Beaufoy Castle.

🌑

And now he sat at a deserted crossroads on a moor, some twenty leagues away from his home; on a horse he had foaled and trained himself; in armour he had hammered out between jobs from metal he paid for. The sword he had strapped around his waist was his ninth effort and possibly the finest of its type in the whole kingdom. Only the sealskin cape, which was safely wrapped in his saddlebag for when it got really cold, was not made by him. That had been a fluttering, tearful gift from the kind Lady Elspeth.

Venn blew on his hands briefly then opened Pail's letter.

> Deare Venn,
> It is time.
>   Pail.

🌑

Venn looked up. In the distance, another rider had just appeared. There was still some mist at the bottom of the muddy valley and the figure took a while to emerge from the gloom as he inexpertly guided his mount in and out of the frozen puddles. To Venn's well-trained eye, the armour the other knight wore had once been of the best quality but had suffered somewhat in the last hundred years or so, from over use and under care. From a distance, he could hear the distinct grating noise of metal on metal and dark patches on the breastplate were almost certainly rust. Strapped to his back was the biggest broadsword Venn had ever clapped eyes on.

'Venn?' Pail looked very little changed – just taller and, if possible, a little thinner. The only marked difference was a certain gangly strength to him as he bought his horse around in a series of strenuous manoeuvres. That done, Pail turned his doleful brown eyes on his friend and did a quick appraisal of his own, remarking inwardly that, in seven years, Venn had become every inch the picture of what a knight should be. 'You look …' he paused, searching for the right word, 'bulky,' he said, giving up eventually.

'I got your letter …' Venn started.

'… and I got your reply,' Pail smiled for the first time, '… otherwise this would have been a pretty big coincidence.' Venn smiled back; this wasn't as awkward as he had feared.

'Did you hear anything from Giff?' Pail asked.

'I got a reply … of sorts … it was mainly pictures.' Venn looked down the hill. 'I'm not sure Giff's quite mastered the art of writing yet.'

'Yeah, I got a letter, too. Quite vivid – Giff's drawing skills – amazing what you can do with purple crayon – lots of red, too, and different ways of expressing how excited he was.'

'Quite.' They both looked down the slope where they expected to see Giff coming along the road. 'I hope he's not late.'

'Oh, he will be.'

Just then, Pail's horse started; he would have bolted if Pail hadn't caught hold of the reins. Something was coming right at them from the rear, through the coppice wood. Judging by the sound of small trees splintering and thickets being roughly thrust aside, it was large and it was coming fast. Venn swung his horse around in one clean movement and drew his sword. Pail struggled somewhat, but eventually got his broadsword free of its sheath. 'Are there still bears in this neck of the woods?' Venn asked.

'Er, yes ... no ... perhaps. Could be a wild boar ... Socrates's got the scent of something and he doesn't like it.' Pail's teeth were gritted with the effort of keeping the huge sword level. Over the noise of undergrowth being crushed, there was another noise that Pail couldn't quite identify at first. D O N G, *oof*, D O N G, *oof*, D O N G, *oof*... it went. A rather large holly bush was all that was now standing between them and whatever was approaching. The bush started to shake as if possessed by wicked spirits and, presently, a ghastly, evil-smelling figure emerged. It was covered from head to foot in mud, or possibly something quite like mud (in consistency and colour) only worse; it had four legs but no discernable head or torso, just a misshapen lump, almost entirely draped with pond weed, creepers, tangles of bramble and bits of tree. A lateral branch from the holly bush flicked back and hit the creature high up, somewhere near where its head should have been. 'D O N G!' went something metal and, '*oof*!' went someone inside it.

'Er, Giff?' said Pail.

'I got lost,' explained Giff as they started to untangle him. 'Hang on a tick,' he struggled with his visor, which wouldn't budge until Venn had a go at it, eventually prising it open with his sword. Then finally, after much more struggling, a familiar face peered out. 'Bloody thing got stuck at

Cirencester. This armour must have shrunk in the wash or something.' Venn raised his eyebrows at Pail – Giff's armour actually seemed to be stretched in places where his stomach was trying hard to burst the iron rivets that kept it together. 'You two look ... blimey, Venn, you're the size of the bear we had for dinner last night! Pail, you're still jolly as ever, come 'ere!' And before either could do anything about it, both boys were grabbed by Giff and treated to a hug.

He smelled absolutely terrible, he looked like a pork sausage squeezed hastily into a metal pipe and he nearly pulled them both out of their saddles but suddenly all three boys felt something they hadn't in seven long years.

They felt at home.

CHAPTER 2
~: Hostile Dave :~

GIFF WAS FILLING THEM IN.

'Well, when I got to Percy's place, I started by helping out in the stables, but horses and I don't seem to get along.' Pail eyed Giff's ride – a sort of giant, very hairy Shetland pony called Knobble that had already tried to bite him twice. 'Next, he tried me in the guard room but I kept falling asleep – I mean, it's very hard staying awake all night, standing about on your tod for hours, staring out at rows of black trees, against a black sky. So I became a footman for a while – liked the uniform but I kept dropping things in the mud, smashing precious ornaments and I can't fold clothes if my life depended on it. Then I was a court jester, but it's hard work being funny on demand and juggling's not as easy as it looks. He's a very patient man, is Percy – never lost his rag for a second.'

'Sounds like a saint,' said Venn, who had the sneaking suspicion that Giff's exile was going to turn out to be a bit of a holiday. He was about to be proved right.

'Finally, he tried me out in the kitchens. And guess what?'

'You set fire to the soup?' suggested Pail, who was thinking along the same lines as Venn.

'... no, I was a natural! Within a week I had been made Percy's Personal Chef. I went everywhere with His Nibs, whipping up omelettes, serving soufflés, grilling, dicing, roasting and baking whatever he managed to shoot. For the first time in my life I was really good at something! In the end I had a small army of sous-chefs and sauce makers working under me. I even invented something to help you eat ... look, I've got one here – even the King uses one – he had it made specially from my prototype …'

'Looks like a half-finished spoon,' observed Pail.

'Not in the least, saves you having to use your fingers to stop your food getting away … I call it a Four-poke, 'cos it's got these four things … for poking ...'

'It'll never catch on.'

Giff waved his hand as if it didn't matter. 'Whatever. Anyway, I'm going to be a knight now. When I got your letter – thanks Pail, by the way – I was super excited, and so was Percy: "It's time we made a knight out of you," he says, all serious-like. "I will put you in the hands of my squire and armourer, they'll get you on the straight and narrow."'

Venn glanced at Giff's badly assembled armour, flapping sword and mismatched gauntlets. 'When was that?'

'Oh, gosh … nearly a week ago.'

Now, a short way off, quite another sort of conversation was in full swing. An argument, in fact.

Four large men, all on foot, were pulling and tugging at a dirty rope as they slipped and skidded their way up a steep bank. The path they were on was well-used and the mud was of the gluey variety that got everywhere and stuck to everything.

'Bloody hoss, stupid nag … I say we kill it, sell the meat at the first place we come to, split the money and go our separate ways.'

'It may be obstinate but that horse alive is still worth more'n a year's wages to the likes of us.'

'You said it was easy money!' said the shortest of the four, looking accusingly at the man at the far end of the rope who he knew only as Hostile Dave.

'It would have been if we'd taken the other path, the one over the hills, but you said this one was quickest – "been using it since I was a nipper," you said. Now if you've got a problem doin' a bit of pulling we can always find a way to cut you out of the deal premature-like.' Dave jabbed a finger threateningly at the man his mother called Timmy, but everyone else knew as Knuckle, on account of a broken nose that resembled a crooked finger.

Knuckle knew a threat when he heard one. He didn't react well to threats, even from large blokes with hands like mallets. 'Oh, yeah, you an' whose mob?'

Hostile Dave didn't even pause as he whipped out a small sword from nowhere and jabbed the blade under Knuckle's Adam's apple. 'Don't need a mob, got this,' he said, grinning viciously through yellow teeth; they were jumbled like broken tombstones and his breath smelled like the grave. 'Lop that ugly nose of yours off in a trice …'

'… an' call it Severance Pay, har, har har,' said the third bloke, who was a friend of the fourth bloke, whose name may have been George or Bill or Daphne for all Dave cared. They'd all met in a tavern with no name and had been drinking hard since the previous day. It was Dave who'd spotted the horse, a beautiful white mare, tall and graceful as a swan being tethered outside the blacksmith's. Nicking her had been relatively easy but he knew they needed to get as far away from the village as possible. A horse of that quality could only have been owned by a Lord or rich knight, and would likely be well known. Twenty miles should do the trick. He couldn't ride, so he'd enlisted the help of his fellow drinkers. This had been a mistake, as it turned out. The mare, beautiful and well-bred as she seemed on the outside, was as obstinate and stupid as any donkey he'd ever encountered.

However, compared to Dave's partners in crime, the horse

was a shining beacon of genius. He planned to get rid of the three of them at the first available opportunity – only he needed them to help get the horse out of range of any search parties. Unfortunately, the effects of all the beer he'd drunk had worn off and bravery and bravado had been replaced by queasiness and a terrible headache. He took a deep breath.

'Now, I suggest we all pull together, get off this road as soon as we can. If we shift, we'll be into the next county before midday. We can get the nag flogged in Redingum and we'll all be rich before nightfall.' He pressed the rusty blade against Knuckle's neck for a few seconds longer – just to make his point – before sheathing it expertly under his ragged cloak and going back to the rope.

He was just about to start pulling again, secure in the knowledge that he had the others' help for at least the next couple of hours, when he heard a cough about ten yards off.

It was actually a polite sounding cough but, nonetheless, there was some authority to it. He looked up and was startled to see a tall, scruffy knight atop a bedraggled horse at the crest of the slope. Behind him, two other shapes he couldn't quite make out through the misty rain looked on. Bloody toffs! Thought Hostile Dave – he was in no mood for this. He decided to ignore the cough (and the toff) and keep going.

'Cough, ahem,' said the cougher.

Right, thought Dave, turning slowly. 'Begging your most 'umble pardon … Suuur,' he fixed the knight with a stare that could wilt roses, 'you seem to 'ave a cold comin' on. I'd best get inside, out of this nasty rain, if I were you.'

'Is that your mare?'

'Prob'ly,' replied Dave in a deliberately insolent way, as if he didn't care whether Pail believed him or not.

'You, Sir, are a liar, I declare. I believe this horse to be stolen. I want your word that it will be returned forthwith to its rightful owner!'

Dave blinked. He actually couldn't quite believe what he was hearing. Ever since he'd left the bloody army, he'd promised himself that no-one would ever get away with speaking to him like that again. But this so-called knight, who, now he'd got up nice and close, turned out to be no more than a boy wearing hand-me-downs, seemed to be oblivious to any of the usual danger signals that Hostile Dave was throwing out. There was only one thing for it. He reached up and grabbed the boy's breastplate with one huge hand and pulled him down so his face was level with the open visor. 'Look, Lord Lahdidah, pink-pansies-grow-around-my-castle, I ain't got time for this or your showin' off in front of your little friends, so, I tell you what, I'll just let me sword do the talking … !'

'What, you're a ventriloquist?' came a muffled voice from the fat one at the back.

Dave's free hand actually got halfway to the hidden scabbard under his cloak when he felt a grip like a boar trap grab his forearm and twist. 'Aaarggh!' he was just about to say before something very hard hit him on the top of his head. His world slipped sideways as he sank into oblivion.

The fight, once it started, lasted no more than a minute. It would have been even quicker, but, halfway through, both Pail and Giff got tangled up in each other's stirrups and Venn had to stop what he was doing (bashing Knuckle about the head with his own lump of wood) and untangle them. 'Best go and catch the mare,' he suggested to the other two, as much to keep them out of the way as to secure the stolen horse who was actually watching the proceedings with a sort of vacant interest – as if this sort of thing happened to her every day.

A few seconds later, Knuckle, like Dave, was out cold.

George (or possibly Daphne) scuttled into the woods with his friend and no-one saw them again.

𝕰𝖁𝕰𝕽.

CHAPTER 3

~: *Stumblefroo-de-Bogge* :~

A SHORT WHILE LATER, Giff, Venn and Pail were being treated to the first hero's welcome they had ever had in their short lives.

The inhabitants of Stumblefroo-de-Bogge rarely had their collection of hovels graced with the presence of a knight – let alone three at once – and these guys had lived up to the villagers' expectations by doing a *Goode Deed* even before they had arrived.

Dirg Bahl – the local farmer, whose horse had been pinched – was immediately fetched. Amidst much clapping and cheering, he grandly invited them all to his *lordy manor* – as he put it – for a *lordy feast* – he added.

Sitting by a roaring fire, listening to Giff recount what had happened, the farmer congratulated himself on how he'd come up in his part of the Wold.

He looked smugly around at his furnishings, all brought with gold he had made himself, through his own hard graft and nose for business – Greek statuettes, Flemish tapestries, gaudy silks from China, Persian rugs and Venetian glasses filled with the best wine from France. The meal had started nearly three hours previously and by now most of the dishes had been brought to the table: lark pie; several plump pigeons cooked in their own blood; a swan, stuffed with a goose, stuffed with a partridge, which, in turn, housed a whole woodcock; and, in the heart of the dish, a delicately par-boiled sparrow. A spit-roasted pig, glazed in honey, studded with cloves and sporting a large cooking apple in its open jaws, formed the centrepiece.

He fancied he was nobody's fool and his hunch had been right – the horse had been worth the hugely inflated price he'd bought it for in the Aqua Sulis auctions. Was he not now hobnobbing with the gentry – even if they were barely adolescents, and the fat one had worse manners than he did? Yup, he'd made it – master of Stumblefroo-de-Bogge today, Falle Down-the-Welle tomorrow!

'How much for that sword of yours?' he said, gesturing with a greasy hand at Venn's weapon, which was hanging up with his belt by the door.

Venn bowed; he knew enough about the type of person the farmer was to suspect that the man would be offended by a flat refusal. 'That thing?' he said, 'It's just a lump of pig iron, blunt as a butter knife.'

The farmer smiled at this. 'You're too modest, young sir – I may be rough but that's quality, always had a nose for it, I could tell a pot pig from a prize porker ever since I was a lad! So, how much? I'll pay more than fair for it.'

'I'm afraid it's not for sale.' Venn's firm tone surprised even Giff, who stopped eating to gawp at the pair.

'Everything's for sale!' declared Farmer Bahl.

Venn attempted to smooth out the scowl that creased his face. The farmer had been more than generous to them. He nodded. 'Probably, but the sword has a job to do – it was made for a purpose and until that duty has been discharged, then only I will wield it.'

'Ah! Revenge, is it, that's got you boys on the road? Well there's no profit in revenge, that's all I can say, but you do what you must,' he paused and took a huge swig of wine. 'Then come back one day and I'll buy that fine piece of workmanship from you.'

Later – much later, in fact – the young guests had retired to the chambers they were sharing. Venn had removed his armour, cleaned it and carefully stowed it under his bed. Then he proceeded to help Giff, who was still struggling to get his breastplate off.

Pail was thinking about the furniture in Bahl's house and just how far they'd all come in a few years. Before he'd left Four Frogs, he would have thought that the feast they had just eaten was the best in the kingdom, not just a bog-standard evening meal for the gentry. The furnishings would have seemed like the height of good taste and fit for any palace, not the gaudy lumps of gilded pine he saw them as now. He sighed – perhaps he'd not learned anything in the last few years. Perhaps he'd just turned into a snob.

Venn was strangely quiet, though.

Giff was making up for it. 'That was so cool Venn – when you picked that guy up with one hand, you should have seen the look on his face, THEN you gave him a brilliant wedgie … when we rode into town like real knights, all those people cheering and saying we were brave and good, and that guy's food … blimey, I must go and see his chef tomorrow and congratulate him … we certainly showed those guys not to mess with us … did you try those strawberries in elder jelly?'

'Yeah, just like real knights,' Venn cut in, using a strangely harsh tone of voice that made Pail look up from his book, 'except we're not, are we?'

'Well, um,' Giff looked a little crestfallen.

'Just because you squeeze yourself into a suit of armour that's two sizes too small for you, you think that makes you a knight, do you?'

'Um …'

'Well, *do* you?'

'Okay, well … I hadn't really … you know … thought …'

'That's it, you're the guy that doesn't think, except about

your stomach, or the next stupid joke you're going to come out with ...'

'Steady on Venn,' said Pail, coming over, 'I think Giff gets the point.' Venn turned angrily to Pail and, for a moment, Pail thought he was going to launch into him. Something cold in Venn's eyes made Pail suddenly slightly afraid of his oldest friend, but he forced himself to stand his ground. The moment – if it could be called that – passed, and imperceptibly some of the warmth returned to Venn's face.

'Sorry,' he said, turning to Giff, 'I didn't mean to have a go at you like that. It's just that putting on this suit of armour, rescuing that horse and everyone thinking we're special just makes me feel worse – like we're fakes. What are we even doing here?'

'We're going back to Four Frogs,' said Giff, without any hesitation and with surprising certainty, 'then we're going to defeat those Iron Knights and put everything back the way it was before.'

'Are we?' Venn shook his head, beginning to look morose again, 'what makes you so sure we can?'

'Because we're in the right!' said Giff, actually sounding more like Venn. The old Venn. Perhaps he's gone for good, thought Pail.

'Look at you, you can't even fight,' but Venn said this gently this time. He was no longer accusing, just stating the obvious.

'But you can teach us!' exclaimed Giff, 'Look, it pains me to say this, but you were brilliant out there and we were rubbish, you're right. But whatever you say, we are basically good, and those Iron Knight thingies are definitely evil; someone's got to stop them and it's our fault that they're there. I'm not stupid, I know I look a bit of an idiot in all this stuff, but you don't. Pail might still have a face like someone's just peed in his tea but he is smart ... we can do this, I know we can.'

Pail smiled and even Venn began to look a bit more cheerful. Each boy was privately remembering how infectious Giff's enthusiasm could be.

Pail ambled over to the window and looked out at the road they would take tomorrow, the old Roman way that eventually led to Four Frogs. He sensed Venn would still need persuading, so he cleared his throat.

'I know we're not knights, not proper ones; we may never yet become them, but we're not really tricking anyone. This armour and these weapons are just tools, aren't they? And, the way I see it, if we need those tools to defeat the Iron Knights, then that's what we have to do.' He turned back to his bed and picked up the book he'd left lying there. 'When I wrote to you both, I didn't tell you about this,' he said, coming over to where Giff and Venn were sitting. 'I thought it might sound stupid and … well, I suppose I wanted to show it to you in person.' Giff made a space for Pail who sat down on the bed and opened the silver bindings on the book.

The Art of Chivalrie was printed in neat gold lettering on the vellum insides. However, instead of turning the first page, Pail slid his finger between the vellum and the leather bindings, opening up a small hidden pocket in the cover. A piece of neatly folded parchment dropped out. Written above the fold were the words,

honos, amicitia, fides.

'I had seen these words before, and I even wrote them down because they seemed important at the time, I don't know why. Then, when I found this sheet of parchment – hidden in the stuffing of the cover of the book I'd been reading – I couldn't believe it. I must have jumped because I knocked the reading candle from its stand; it fell right out of the window. I didn't care though, it was a full moon, so I ran outside and read what it said.' Pail held the old piece of parchment up to the candlelight so Venn and Giff could see what was written. The page was old, clearly much older than the book itself, but whoever had concealed it in the secret pocket had done so carefully because, although the writing was ancient, it was still clear enough to read.

Knightes who must united be
Against the gravest adversity
Vanquish with honour, friendship and loyalty
Only then will one be three
- honos, amicitia, fides -

Venn actually smiled but all his harshness and sarcasm had gone. 'Are you saying that we're meant to be these three knights?'

'Of course!' exclaimed Pail with uncommon passion, 'If we want to be. I've looked up *honos, amicitia, fides*. No noble family has had it as their motto – ever – it could be ours!'

'OK,' said Venn slowly, 'so this thing you found is like a prophecy, and if we fight under this motto …'

'I honestly don't know but it's a coincidence, at the very least. And Giff's right … we can defeat them, we can do it!' cried Pail, thumping Venn on the arm good-naturedly, who responded by pushing Pail off the bed with a mock growl. Giff, always quick to join in a play fight, jumped on Venn's back who laughed as he struggled to get him off. Feeling lighter than he had in years, Pail switched allegiance and gave Giff a dead leg.

Five minutes later, all three were on the floor, rolling around in a messy heap. Dirg's butler bustled in to see what all the noise was about.

'It's alright, all sorted – just bats!' said Venn, out of breath and laughing as he leapt up and into bed in a single bound.

'Seems they've flown off now,' remarked Pail to Giff as he dusted himself off.

'Worth checking under the beds like that, though, good thinking – you never know,' said Giff airily, giving the butler his best smile.

They're just kids! The old butler shook his head and the door closed, leaving the boys in darkness.

'OK, so now we just need a plan,' declared Giff to no-one in particular.

Chapter 4
~: *Training* :~

The next morning, after profuse thanks and goodbyes had been exchanged, Giff loaded up with leftovers and they set out.

It would take them over three weeks to get home.

The rest of the journey was hard – mainly thanks to Venn. They slept out in the open, rising just before dawn, whereupon Venn would make Giff and Pail join him to wash in the nearest freezing stream. When Giff wasn't looking, Venn had also thrown all of the greasy leftovers that he had procured from Dirg straight into a ditch; they were forced to live off wild berries and the occasional lean hare they managed to trap.

After their swim, Venn would tutor his friends for an hour in swordplay.

'It's all about balance,' he would insist, over and over again, as they repeated the same movements until both were ready to drop down with exhaustion. 'Lose your footing and you're dead.' Often, he would give Giff a shove, who almost always fell over with a shout of annoyance. 'Balance and speed! Learn the moves; practise until you can do them even if you're only half alive.' And so they learned the cuts, the thrusts, the parries and the hacking that all knights had to master.

At first Pail could hardly lift his massive sword. Giff complained pretty much all the time about blisters. But Venn just forced Pail to work even harder on his upper body strength, and put a horrible paste of charcoal and dung on Giff's hands until he shut up about them.

After working on their swordsmanship they would have

a cold breakfast of whatever leftovers remained from the night before. Venn would tie Socrates and Knobble to Havoc and ride slightly ahead of his friends who, stripped down to the waist in spite of the cold, ran panting behind for mile after mile over hilly, wet, stony, muddy, bleak, horrible countryside.

Giff genuinely thought that Venn had turned into some kind of sadist and that they would both die of exhaustion before he was through with them. But Pail, who had got used to this new, more serious Venn, could see the benefits; certainly in Giff, who had lost so much weight he now looked pretty good in his armour. As for Pail, his arms, which had carried nothing heavier than books for seven years, became knotted with sinewy muscle. After two weeks, he could wield his sword with a fluidity and speed that would not have disgraced a fully trained knight.

'Been meaning to ask you – what's that?' enquired Giff one morning as he watched Venn strap his sword back onto Havoc after a particularly gruelling session. Giff was pointing at the hilt of the weapon and a curious series of metal loops that wound around the base of the finger guard. Venn stopped what he was doing and handed his broadsword to Giff who took it in both hands with a surprised grunt.

'It's something I made myself,' he said with an uncharacteristic hint of pride in his voice. 'I call it a blade breaker.' He took the sword back from Giff. 'Look, I'll show you. Draw your sword.' Giff did as he was asked and assumed a fighting stance. 'Right, now come at me as if you mean it.'

Giff thought of all those cold baths and terrible meals. 'No problem,' he said between gritted teeth.

Their blades met with a loud clang that made Pail look up and draw closer. Giff swung and Venn blocked easily for half a dozen moves. Then, as Giff lunged forward, his blade pointing low, Venn lunged too, instead of parrying, and jinked his arm at the last moment. Pail saw it immediately – Giff's blade had become trapped in the nest of twisting metal around Venn's hilt. Giff tugged, but his sword was firmly stuck. He frowned and tugged harder, but Venn, smiling now, just gripped tighter.

'All, I need to do now is give a good twist and your blade will snap in half,' he said. Giff looked briefly alarmed then relaxed as Venn jinked his own sword and freed Giff's blade. Pail couldn't help but be impressed. 'I have a feeling that blade breaker thing could catch on.'

❧

As they neared their destination, Giff no longer had to be booted awake by Venn – two mornings in a row, he was even up and bathed first before Venn had time to put on the thick woollen shirt that went underneath his own chain mail. Instead of gasping for air like he was a large halibut out of water and just about to die, he now laughed and talked as he ran. The last days of their journey flew by – and then one evening, Rainbeard's Castle finally appeared on the far horizon.

They stood staring at it for several minutes in silence, lost in their own thoughts.

'It'll be just like the welcome we got at that last place – only way better … there'll be people cheering and dancing about, party hats and cake … I'm positive there'll be cake,' Giff was happily munching on a hare's leg, talking with his mouth full as they looked at the dying sun, reflecting pink and mauve on the Castle.

'I guess so,' said Venn but not very convincingly. To Pail, who had seen glimpses of his childhood friend returning over the past few weeks, he seemed to be not so much withdrawn as nervous. Pail could sympathise with this; whilst the Castle looked beautiful from a distance, it also seemed somehow remote and cold – very much like the memories of his old life.

Oh, lighten up, he suddenly thought in a moment of self-awareness. Everyone in Four Frogs was practically related – of course they'd be pleased to see them, they were family. The sun had gone behind the trees now and the darkness was gathering around the corners of the field in which they camped. He stretched out and closed his eyes. It would be fine.

And when Pail awoke early in the morning and smelled the cooking fires from his old village, he smiled. He even had the beginnings of a plan.

CHAPTER 5
~: A Good Decision :~

FROBISHER HAD BEEN in a worse mood than usual all week. Poor Chaffinch was back in the library and looking more terrified by the minute. He ducked as a book on Latin syntax whistled past his head and sailed out of the window. 'I can't find anything in here anymore!' his lord and master bellowed, rummaging through piles of scrolls and vellum parchments. 'If only …' he stopped.

Chaffinch knew what he'd been about to say: if only Pail had been there, he'd have known where to find whatever tome it was he was looking for. Since the boy had left, however, Frobisher had avoided mentioning the boy by name. Chaffinch lowered his head – he felt sorry for the old knight – perhaps Cook was right. 'He's grievin',' she said that morning over hot porridge. 'That boy meant the world to him.'

❧

A hundred miles away, Percival was mooning around his own castle. He spent some time in the Longroom but couldn't find anything there to interest him and so, finally, he drifted into the kitchens. After about ten minutes, the cook began to get annoyed; he always seemed to be standing just where she wanted to be doing something, so she shooed him out. No-one seemed to be in the guardroom and the stables were also deserted. Percival stood staring out the window for a long while. Then, sighing, he eventually went back to the Longroom.

Both knights would have been less out of sorts had they known that – almost at that precise minute – Sir Godfrey was sending out messengers to each of them.

CHAPTER 6

~: Four Frogs Revisited :~

EVERYWHERE THERE WAS MUD.

Churned by countless feet and hooves, it had mixed with human waste from the ditches, which in turn spilled over and washed down dark excrement from the sheep: miserable-looking creatures that had been corralled either side of what had once been the main square.

What was left of the pond was now a quicksand of sewage covered in a dense, black layer of dead flies.

Giff moved Knobble to avoid a sprawling pile of wizened turnips that was quietly rotting from the bottom up and did his best to ignore the smell.

Something wasn't right. Correction: nothing was right.

It was late evening and, as they had slowly made their way during the afternoon down into the hidden valley that had once been their home, the temperature had gradually dropped and the ambient light dimmed. The horses, feeling as if the narrow sides of the valley were closing in on them – like a trap – had tossed their heads and sidestepped their way along the overgrown track that meandered down to the village. Even Havoc had to be gently coaxed by Venn for the last mile.

By now, they were in the centre of the village, but there was still no sign of life. They had not drawn their swords, but they had lowered their helms for safety. The small, but once cheerful cottages that had lined the main square now appeared to be empty; many of them had partially collapsed thatch roofs and doors hanging off their hinges. Pail was beginning to think that the village was deserted – imagining that everyone had simply packed up one day and gone away without leaving a forwarding address.

Then he heard a small sound.

At first he couldn't identify what it was or where it came from but as he rounded the corner, slightly ahead of his two friends, he saw a thin girl. She was standing about halfway up the main street that led towards the Castle. Her ragged dress was hemmed with mud and she was crying quietly to herself as she attempted to comfort – or perhaps gain comfort from – a doll that was made of nothing more than brittle sticks tied together with twine.

When she heard the approach of the horses she looked up, her eyes very large and afraid.

'Wait!' shouted Pail; but with his visor down, his voice sounded inhuman and booming from inside its metal casing. The little girl shot a look of utter terror backwards at them as she ran barefoot through the sea of mud up the road. Pail followed her progress as she disappeared through a narrow gap in a bristling wall of freshly cut wooden stakes that now stood where the church had once been.

The three friends kicked their horses and trotted up to the rough fence that, as they got closer, turned out to be the only wall of a small round stockade. To Pail, it looked like it was designed more to keep people in than out – like a prison – and he was surprised when he heard someone shout. 'Who's there, what do you want from us?'

Venn kicked Havoc forward. 'We are travellers; we only want shelter. We have our own food.'

After some heaving, the wicker gate swung open and a grey haired man with a pronounced stoop came out. He looked surprised at the three knights on horseback and took an involuntary step back, wiping his hands on his coarse hair shirt.

'My Lord,' said the man, 'I apologise, I can see now why the little girl thought you were …' he paused and looked at a loss, 'well … she thought you were someone else, she got afraid … although you look to be goodly knights, who would mean no common folk any harm.' Pail stared at the man through his visor, recognition rendering him speechless. By now, other people had begun to appear behind him; pinched, dirty faces peered out of the gaps in the wooden stakes that made up the walls of the compound. The man looked embarrassed. 'However, I should warn you, this is a sad place. I'm ashamed to say we have little to offer you by way of comfort.' Behind his helmet, Pail felt his eyes prick with tears.

'Dad,' he said, finally raising his visor.

When Simon looked up and saw his son, he seemed to stagger as if someone had suddenly loaded his shoulders with heavy stones.

'Who is it?' cried a woman near the back of the crowd. 'Who comes to us at this time? They must be up to no good.'

'It's my son,' said Simon in little more than a whisper, then stronger. 'My son!' A smile lifted his features to something approaching that Pail remembered; something he had dreamed about when he was missing home all those nights when he was younger.

Sensing what he thought was a change in the atmosphere Giff also raised his visor. 'And it's me, too! Giff! Has anyone one seen my …' but he didn't get any further, as a turnip struck the side of his cheek, followed by a rock. Luckily, the rock missed its intended target, glancing off the top of Giff's helm.

'It's them!' shouted the same woman, 'those bloody brats what have done this to us! Come back to gloat, no doubt, and all lahdi-dah, I see! Atop their fancy horses, pretending to be knights whilst we wallow in misery!'

By now, there was a hubbub of people crowding around the gate; they were eyeing the unexpected visitors, their whispers turning into jeers. Someone grabbed the reins of Socrates, trying to drag him into the compound. Pail was instantly reminded of the night they had admitted what they had done, all those years ago. The frightened villagers had turned on them then. And, like last time, they were saved by the only authority still recognised in the village.

'Stand back!' came the unmistakable, gravelled voice of Stirn. 'Step aside! And that means you too, Mistress Con – and I would put that rock down before someone gets hurt. Is this the way we greet travellers now, who come to Four Fro-?' but the words died on his lips as he found himself looking into the face of his son.

CHAPTER 7

~: *Grim News* :~

IT WAS FAR WORSE than they'd ever imagined.

Half an hour later, they were seated on the bare earth floor of the hall where the villagers now ate and slept and pretty much lived on top of one another – when they weren't working like slaves.

None of the other villagers may have seemed pleased to see them, but Venn, Giff and Pail's parents were overjoyed. It was a long time before any of the boys could get them to stop smothering them with hugs, clapping them on the back whilst dabbing their eyes with dirty rages that had once been hankies. All overjoyed, that is, except for Stirn, who sat a little apart from the family groups, looking at the boys, his expression closed, unreadable. Venn found himself glancing across to his dad, who would meet his gaze for the briefest of moments then turn away.

'What's happened to the village?' asked Giff. 'Why are all the houses so broken down and deserted? Why is everyone in here – it's horrible?' Giff's mother, Didee – her once red hair now snow-white and her naturally round, freckled face thin and lined – stopped smiling.

'Oh, son, you always did ask the silliest of questions. That's all because of Them – who else? Those so-called Iron Knights, those abominations from the Castle! They won't let us live in our homes no more and they forced us to build this.' She gave her surroundings a contemptuous gesture.

'For seven years we've all been moving rocks, digging ditches and shovelling earth one way and then the other and still none of it makes any sense to us. We're not building anything. No sooner have we dug some hole in the ground then the tall one, Bane – he's evil, the worst of the three of them – barks, slashes and terrifies us all until we fill it in again. Then he makes us move onto the next hole or ditch. We've no tools or time to make them. Everything you see has all been gouged and dug out of the dead earth with our bare hands. It's only at night, when They've gone back to that castle of theirs and when most of us are too tired to stand, that we can creep out and sow a few seeds and tend to what's left of the flocks, or we'd starve!'

Pail let his head hang – in part because he felt suddenly very tired and partly because he couldn't bear to look around the room anymore. It had been much worse than he'd expected and, seeing it all – the mud, the misery and the stench of over-crowding – he couldn't come to terms with how the villagers now lived and, worse, how sad and stooped – broken – his parents had become. He felt shocked, angry and bewildered. 'But there must be some reason for all of this, surely?'

But Didee just shook her head. 'See that sign?' she said, pointing to a large slab of oak that had the message *work, power, service* scorched into the wood in foot high gouges, '– the mad one, Squawk you called 'im on the first day, and the name stuck – well he scratched that with that spear of 'is. It's all they care about, forcing their will on us, making us do their bidding, like we was beasts of burden – no better than dumb oxen who pull a cart with no idea why until they become too weak and are slaughtered for dog food.'

Pail moved his head from side to side as if scanning the floor for something. This was all their fault. 'Can't you just escape?' he asked in the end. At these words several of the other villagers who were in earshot – those that were either staring at Pail, Venn and Giff, or slouching against the walls, half-asleep – looked up, suddenly agitated.

'No!' Pail's mother looked panicked too. 'Don't ever say

that word! They seem to know when one of us tries to. There are …' she looked around before continuing in a half-whisper, '… spies for *Them*. Some of the villagers have turned against their own. They'll let Bane know if anyone is planning to escape, or even if someone says they're going to refuse to work or stand up to them; then, the next day, Bane will get Bludge to hurt whoever it was in some way. They'll know you're here by now …' she trailed off, looking worn out by her own words and close to tears at the thought of what might happen.

'Every day is the same, seven days a week. They come down the hill at dawn and that Bludge rouses us by banging on that huge metal disk you saw hanging by the gate. We have barely time for a drink of water before It gets impatient and comes in to start knocking us about – even the women and children. It broke young Ribie's arm last week – you remember her – the Jonas' youngest – she's only ten. Now she's sick and so thin, but she still has to get up and work. These Iron Knights will kill us all eventually. Oh!'

Didee looked at them with tears in her pale grey eyes. 'You should never have come back!'

But Giff shook his head emphatically, grasping his mother firmly by the shoulders. 'Don't worry Mum – look at us, we're almost fully trained knights – Venn here could fight anyone …'

'Any*one* may as be but not any*thing*.' Stirn seemed to rouse himself. He looked hard at each of the boys in turn, taking in their armour and swords. Pail suddenly felt ridiculous, like they had been caught dressing up and were too old for such games. Stirn looked longest and hardest at his son, although Pail noted that Venn now returned his father's sword-sharp gaze without faltering – something no-one else in the village could do. 'Bane or Bludge will come down tomorrow,' he said, 'and batter all three of you into the mud right before our eyes. There won't be a man in the village who can stop Them.' He turned his head and raised his voice to a shout. 'And some of you here will look at it as good sport and shame on you – but I know who you are and one day there'll be a reckoning!' The boys looked around the room and noticed a few faces colour and eyes go shifty. Stirn now looked back at Venn.

'We sent you away for a reason all those years ago – to save you – and it broke your mothers' hearts, but you're alive and you've been treated well as far as I can see – better'n we'd expected,' Stirn shook his head, before correcting himself – he'd never expected anything out of life he hadn't worked for, 'better than we *hoped* for. And so I won't allow you to stay and be killed.' Then he got up to go. Just before he got to the door he turned around. 'I'm pleased to see you all, it gladdens my heart, especially to see my son, Venn has grown up so … fine. But you *will* leave tomorrow an hour before dawn.' He opened the door.

'Before *They* come!'

Chapter 8
~: *Bludge* :~

Outside the compound there was nothing – just freezing black fog, no shadows, no light and no sound. Everything that lay beyond the flimsy walls might as well be deep in the frozen reaches of space, as if the village and all those in it were somehow cast away – adrift in a void of billowing black mists.

Nevertheless, someone was watching.

By and by, It detached from the shadows – a darker mass than the rest, moving slowly and silently through the thick fog towards where the exhausted men, women and children slept fitfully.

Bludge could now tread with a lightness of step almost as that of his master, Bane. Cold fury burned in his iron flanks for the intrusion. The boy-knights' arrival had been reported almost at once. In a few moments, he would be inside the compound and the killing would begin.

Then.

Despite having no feelings to speak of, he almost yelped with surprise when someone stepped out from nowhere and hit him with more force than he had felt in the whole of his existence.

At that moment, on either side of the square, firebrands suddenly flared. The tar was lit, forming an ovular pool of swirling, foggy light – like an arena.

Fully armoured, Venn looked dispassionately at Bludge, who was lying on the muddy ground. His metal heels scrabbled for purchase as he tried to right himself, like some terrible, giant bug. Venn grunted with grim satisfaction – he had known they wouldn't wait for morning. Both Pail and Giff, who now held the burning torches aloft, had agreed, so they began to lay their trap as soon as the other villagers had settled down for the night, stealing out into the dark, fully armed.

Venn tossed the now bent lamp iron onto the ground beside the Knight. 'Your time has come,' he said brusquely, 'I am calling you out, Iron Knight.' And with that he turned and marched calmly back to where Havoc waited.

Still trying to get up, it took a few seconds for Bludge to process what had just happened and what had just been said to him. No-one had hit him before – some had tried, but none had actually made contact, and he had certainly never been felled. None had challenged him so openly either and calmly walked away. He experienced something that a human would have described as rage burning in his stomach, as if a dry furnace had somehow sprung to life in his bowels. 'WHOARRRGH, GHAAAR!' he cried, as he finally managed to get to his feet. He searched around, angrily scanning the swirling red fog and saw Venn mounting his horse. 'GHAAARGGHH!' he bellowed, banging his huge mace against his chest, which boomed like a steel drum as Venn swung Havoc around, lowered his lance and charged. 'I BLARDGE!' screamed the Iron Knight now, charging towards his enemy.

Astride Havoc, Venn was almost the same height as his opponent. Despite this, he was still dwarfed by Bludge's bulk. If It was in the least concerned by the thundering hooves and the vicious-looking lance, It didn't show it. When the two met, knight against Knight, each was almost at full speed. The sound was deafening – splintering wood and the sound of metal being crushed and torn. Pail, watching intently from the sidelines, couldn't help but wince. Bludge roared again, though whether in fury or pain it was hard to tell as Venn emerged from a dense cloud of fog, still on his horse but visibly shaken, his lance broken in half, the stump split down the middle. He tossed it aside and drew his sword.

'Venn!' shouted Pail in warning as Bludge burst out of the fog before the boy had a chance to wheel Havoc around for a second pass. The Iron Knight had a large rent torn in his breastplate that would have surely meant certain death for anyone else. But Bludge seemed undamaged and his smashed armour did not seem to be slowing him down in the least.

He hit Havoc broadside, the horse's whinny turning into a shriek as his ribs were crushed. Nevertheless, Havoc was a warhorse; his sinuous heart was the size of one of Bludge's fists, and he wasn't beaten yet. He reared up, his forelegs pummelling the air in an attempt to strike at his attacker's head. In retaliation, Bludge hit him again, this time with his mace. It knocked Havoc sideways, unhorsing Venn, who fell and rolled.

The battered horse fell and lay quite still on the ground. Pail almost ran forward at this point, his own sword half-drawn, but Venn was on his feet in an instant, his sword still in his hand. Bludge put his head down and charged again – mace swinging, drawing complicated figures-of-eight in the air.

Luckily, Venn was much too fast and he sidestepped, allowing his much bigger opponent to pass by before he struck. The blow was very fast but not quite high enough and it glanced off Bludge's coif, the metal strip that protected the back of his huge neck. Bludge turned and charged again. Venn sidestepped and swung once more, his blow glancing off again.

And so it went on: charge, side step; occasionally Bludge would swing his mace and Venn would parry, make a useless attempt to pierce his opponent's armour, followed by another charge from Bludge and so on. All of the villagers were up by now, crowding about the edges of the illuminated fog, watching in virtual silence. The initial awe and hope to see someone finally standing up to – and matching – one of the Iron Knights blow for blow began to fade as they could see Venn tiring. Venn's mother looked terrified, his father resigned.

That's it, thought Pail, standing on his own at the edge of the arena; I've got to go in and help him.

He stepped forward, but instantly felt something on his neck. The blade was cold, as if the metal had been encased in permafrost, and it was so unnaturally sharp that, with only the slightest pressure exerted, he still felt his own blood well around his Adam's apple and trickle warmly down his neck.

Pail looked up into the twin coals of Bane's eyes.

The tall, almost impossibly black Knight must have moved with the speed and quietness of a shadow to have got this close without Pail noticing. He could have easily cut Pail's throat there and then but it was clear that his only interest was in keeping him distracted from the fight.

'Baaa'k!' Pail swivelled his eyes in the other direction and noticed Squawk step into the fray. 'BAA'K!' This wasn't good. Venn was just about holding his own, but if Squawk joined in, the fight would be over in seconds. He needn't have worried, though. With a shout that was shrill compared to Bludge but at least sounding human, Giff ran forward, brandishing his broadsword. 'Aaarrrkkk?!' cried the beaked knight in surprise.

Giff came in hard and very fast, making a series of attacking strokes that Pail recognised as moves that Venn had taught them both. Squawk reeled at the onslaught and, for a moment, it looked as if Giff might score a quick, almost miraculous victory. Unfortunately, Squawk began to fight back with a series of eccentric but quite effective wild jabs with the spear he was carrying. Giff, who stood at least two feet smaller than his opponent, had to keep ducking to avoid being skewered like a large metal kebab, and this dulled the speed of his attack.

The villagers were transfixed, looking from one fight to another, not quite sure where each was going.

But just when things seemed perfectly even between all four knights – when there still seemed hope – disaster struck.

Venn had been circling the arena, using his greater skill and speed to avoid Bludge. Provided he didn't tire too much, he still stood a chance of finally striking a blow that would find the crucial gap in Bludge's armour. But the longer they fought, the more slippery the mud became. And then the inevitable happened.

Venn slipped.

As he fell, Bludge let out a reverberating bellow of victory and stepped forward, kicking Venn's sword out of his hand. He dug the heel of his metal boot into Venn's stomach, crushing him into the ground, and raised his mace.

This was it. Pail, seeing that Venn had lost, and knowing that with Bane's sword pressing at his throat he could do nothing, uttered a thin cry of despair.

Just then, he heard a snort; he spun around to see Havoc, eyes rolling, flanks bleeding, power out of the fog and barrel into Bludge. Even Bludge couldn't withstand the full force of Havoc's charge this time, and he fell sideways as the warhorse carried on, finally crumpling at the ragged line of villagers who could see he had used the last of his energy in this one, life-saving charge.

But it was enough. Venn was back on his feet and now he held his sword aloft above the writhing form of Bludge who, for the moment at least, could not raise himself. 'See this –

creature – my broadsword.' Venn pulled his helm off with his spare hand; his hair was matted with sweat and his breath came out in gasps but he was filled with a strange confidence. 'I made this sword; I smelted the ore, beat the metal and honed the blade. Into it I have put my blood, sweat and perhaps even part of my soul.' He paused as Bludge finally hauled himself to his feet, growling low, deep in his huge chest. Venn smiled, he could have finished Bludge off on the ground but it was not the honourable thing to do. Now Bludge was on his feet again, the fight was fair. 'But this sword is just a tool, when all is said and done – man made, as are you and therefore, when it is no longer of any use, man broken.' He pointed the tip of his sword at the Iron Knight. 'Like you!'

If Bludge understood, he didn't show it, but for once, he was silent. Turning, he swung his mace with more grace and speed than he'd shown so far, and it thrummed through the air.

Unbelievably, as the terrible weapon honed in on its target, Venn stayed perfectly still. Until the very last moment. Only then did he duck forward, allowing the heavy mace to pass within less than the thickness of a butterfly wing from the back of his head. Then he arched his back as the mace came around again on the backswing, pummelling the air where his jaw had been less than a second before. As the mace missed, Bludge roared in frustration and Venn now rocked forward on his heels, still perfectly balanced, his sword singing as it sliced through the fog.

All his strength must have gone into the blow because the blade hit Bludge's coif, cutting through it like it was tin, connecting with the rings of iron that wound around his neck, slicing through those too, and through the metal tendons, the wires and finally the iron vertebrae.

With a roar cut short by Venn's blade, Bludge's torso, now

separated from the huge head, stood for a second, tried to turn one way, swayed, turned another and then crumpled at the knees. The huge iron head fell into the mud and rolled to the edge of the crowd.

Squawk looked up with a cry of alarm and Giff seized his chance, bringing his own sword down on Squawk's head, as if to slice it in two, down the middle. The move was effective but Squawk was quick and he drew back just in time – Giff's blade cutting a deep groove in his crown but not going all the way.

Bane made an odd noise in the back of his throat. He turned to Pail, his red eyes seeming to flare, and pulled the sword away from Pail's throat. Stepping backwards, he disappeared into the fog. Before Giff could react, Squawk followed fast, wires fizzing from the top of his head as he disappeared into the night.

❦

For a few moments, there was no noise. Then, slowly, one by one, the villagers began to clap and then to cheer, some of the braver children even approaching Bludge to prod his metal remains before scampering back to their parents.

❦

Chapter 9
~: *Celebration* :~

THE NEXT MORNING, no Iron Knights came down the hill.

For the first time in seven long years, the inhabitants of Four Frogs – the sheep and Mistress Moon's donkey included – actually had something to celebrate after a good lie-in.

A short while after the dawn appeared on the horizon – in the form of a grey, whirling mist that turned pink as the sun rose and burned away the remnants of the previous night's dense fog – the villagers slowly emerged. Each was drawn towards the remains of the Iron Knight, as if they needed re-assurance that the battle at midnight had really taken place and wasn't merely a happy dream.

Havoc lay a little way off. When Stirn came out of the compound, he was surprised to see his son kneeling by the great, proud beast. He must have been there all night; his armour was frost-tinged and he looked exhausted. The Headman was also surprised that Havoc still seemed to be clinging on to life. Venn glanced up when his father approached. 'He'll be alright,' he said, somewhat defensively. Everyone knew that injured horses were put down after battle.

Stirn examined the warhorse, noticing the matted blood, how shallow his breathing was, and the way the whites of his eyes showed. Froth around his mouth was flecked red. Stirn shook his head. It was a shame – he was a brave beast, and no mistake.

'I will do it, if you like, son.'

'No,' insisted Venn. After what he had done the night

before, no-one – not even his father – had the heart to argue.

So Stirn, Farn, Venn, Pail and several others, including Giff, gently lifted Havoc onto a pallet and dragged him into the compound. Father Mally, who had taken on the role of physician since his church had been destroyed, said he'd do his best for him. 'He's one of God's creatures and we all owe him deep gratitude.' At this short speech, Venn had looked more grateful than he could probably put into words.

❧

Then a celebration began, muted at first, but slowly building into something more joyful and abandoned as the villagers shrugged off seven hard years of fear and soul-destroying labour.

Pail, Giff, and several other villagers heaved Bludge's iron remains to the edge of the village, where the road carried on up to the Castle. Venn led the way, hefting the huge head in both hands. Then they chopped a rowan down and lit a fire, watching as the metal went from black to red as the green wood burned with searing intensity. They didn't care that Bludge was unlikely to disappear to melt away; only that the flames seemed to be scorching his memory, cauterising the harm he had wrought on the village for all those years.

Maisy then asked Ma Windy to cook several of her older hens in a huge pot with some of Father Mally's wine. Even Cobb donated two fine suckling pigs to honour the first feast the village had enjoyed together for years. As the pigs sizzled mouth-wateringly on a spit, Farn Jr. and Starl – Giff's older brothers – gave each other a look and sloped off. They came back a few minutes later, covered in straw, waving two huge flagons of cider they'd hidden when the trouble began.

The boys, especially Venn, got the welcome now that Giff had so wanted; Pail still feeling undeserving, Venn embarrassed and Giff grinning like the top of his head was about to come off as they received claps on the back from the men, hugs from the women and various home-made gifts that weren't always easy to identify from small children.

Cobb approached the boys as they sat under a tree. They were each tucking into a huge lump of pork and crackling as he summed it up. 'We were angry about what you'd done, but I'm ashamed for the way we treated you. You were just boys, after all. It could have been any one of us when we were your age. Got close to going up to the Castle once or twice myself,' he winked, his weathered face creasing, 'as did your dad, if I remember right!'

Pail did notice that two people were avoiding the festivities. Brother Pike and Mistress Pittle stood as far away from the fire as possible, both looking uncomfortable and, if he wasn't mistaken, a little afraid.

Any other thoughts along those lines were derailed, however, as a great shout came up from the compound and the crude sign – *work, power, service* – was unceremoniously pulled down and dumped on the fire.

Some of the villagers began to gather up their few belongings from the compound and take them back to their empty cottages. Doors were nailed back on hinges, thatch hastily re-stuffed and patched, hearths swept and fires lit. Pail looked around and smiled, then laughed for joy.

It was Giff who eventually discovered why Brother Pike and Mistress Pittle had not been taking part in the celebrations. He was so full of pork, chicken and cider that he needed somewhere to have a little lie down. Since his vigorous training, his appetite – or at least his capacity to consume trough-sized quantities of food and lakes of drink – had all but disappeared, along with his stomach and most of his backside. Though proud of the new muscular Giff, he was nostalgic for the days when he thought nothing of chomping through enough food to feed a small horse.

Another symptom of his new look seemed to be girls. All of that morning, Soozie Brick had been making strange faces at him. Initially, Giff had assumed it was indigestion, something he'd had his fair share of experience with, and so he gave her sympathetic looks back. Far from making things better, this seemed to bring on even more rolling eyes and spasms. 'There'll be a wedding afore Whitsun,' muttered Granny Avfeldig as she hobbled by – much to Giff's alarm.

'I'm only fifteen,' he protested.

'So?' said Granny without a backward glance. Giff felt hot and cold.

Soozie Brick was best described as homely, but she did have a certain way about her. It was a forwardness that Giff suddenly found disconcerting and attractive all at the same time.

⚜

Anyway, all but staggering his way towards the large barn, where he was sure he would find a nice quiet corner in which to hide, hopefully with some warm hay to lie down on, Giff heard a noise.

He turned and was surprised to see his older brother Starl and several other young men about the same age – many who looked familiar but whose names he couldn't quite remember. The Pittle woman and Brother Pike had their backs to the wall and his older brother formed the centre of a threatening-looking semi-circle around them.

Mistress Pittle looked scared but defiant; Brother Pike looked very close to tears. Starl turned.

'Better move along there Bro. This 'ere's village business.'

Giff, feeling much less sleepy all of a sudden, found Pail and Venn sitting by the embers of the fire. 'Er, guys, I think you'd better come and have a word before my brother does something stupid.'

They met Starl and his gang returning across the courtyard. The young clergyman and Wednesday Pittle were now tightly bound by their wrists, dragged along by a snarling Starl. Brother Pike slipped and fell and was being yanked to his feet when Venn stepped forward and placed himself in front of Starl. He stood almost a head taller than him. 'What is going on here?' he asked firmly but as respectfully as possible.

Starl glared at Venn. 'Like I said to our kid, stay out of this, 'tis village business.'

'Whatever's coming to them, they deserve it!' Didee, Giff's mum, had seen what was happening and had rushed over; more villagers were arriving all the time. 'They betrayed us to those monsters,' she continued. 'Always scampering up to the Castle, like we didn't know, tellin' them so-called Knights what was goin' on. It was Wednesday 'ere what prob'ly told 'em youz was all back and where to find youz.'

'Nevir got no 'elp from you when I was on me own, nevir got no 'elp when the Iron Masters came – so what choice did I 'ave? I ain't got no 'usband to look aftir me!' Mistress Pittle spat back. A chorus of angry voices ran through the gathering crowd at this.

'They should be punished!'

'Let Starl an' his lot do what they were gonna do, no

questions asked!'

'Burn 'em!'

'Yeah, fry 'em with Bludge!'

'Noooo!' Brother Pike fell to his knees, crying. 'I'm sorry, forgive me ... I was afraid ... I thought I could help – after the church was smashed, I thought there was no stopping them, that these were the Devil's creatures – and I was weak, I thought we could make things better if we served them faithfully ... I thought ...'

'What a coward, he's worse than that Pittle. Burn 'im first!'

'No burn 'er first. Make 'im watch! He'll hate that.'

'No!' shouted Giff, 'Have you all gone insane? What's wrong with this village? Before we left, no-one got punished like this, there were no burnings. What have these Iron Knights done to you?'

'Exactly,' cried someone, 'you don't know, cos you weren't there!'

Giff's response was to step forward and draw his sword halfway out of its leather scabbard. 'No-one lays a finger on them!'

A few of the villagers took a pace back but Starl just shook his head. 'You can't fight all of us.'

Stirn now moved through the crowd. He reached forward and grabbed the twine that Starl was using to drag the two prisoners. 'No-one is getting burned today, nor any other day.' There was a wall of protest at this.

'BUT!' the protests flared up, 'These two are traitors! They have done wrong and they deserve to be punished ...'

'Wait!' Pail addressed the crowd now. 'This is wrong. If there's one thing I've learned today and not out of a book, for once, then its forgiveness. We went to the Castle, we woke the Knights and yet you, all of you, forgave us for that today – this great morning – and everyone pulled together to start rebuilding the village we love. Wednesday and Brother Pike both acted out of nothing more than fear – fear that we have all felt – and anyone who denies that is a liar. Brother Pike was misguided, but he's admitted that he thought he was helping; Wednesday here is on her own, and, quite understandably, she felt that she had to ally herself with the strongest to survive. Let us not forget for one moment, our *real* enemies are the Iron Knights!'

There were a few murmurs of agreement and some people began to look less sure of themselves.

'If this village is to be rebuilt amidst the spilled blood of its inhabitants and founded on feelings of recrimination and of bitter vengeance, then that is a village I, for one, no longer want to be a part of!'

'Hear, hear!' Terence knew a bandwagon when he saw one coming. However, some of the villagers, especially Starl and his friends, looked annoyed.

Pail licked his lips. 'We've not won yet and we're going to lose if we fight on their terms. Even if we win, we'd have lost the part of ourselves that makes us different from those abominations. We call them knights, but the quality of a knight is not strength, nor the wielding of power, nor making others work,' he pointed at the charred sign: 'but mercy …' Pail closed his eyes, visualising the scroll he must have read a hundred times,' – *for mercy bears fruits far greater than that of stricte justice*. If we punish Brother Pike and Wednesday Pittle that's two less people we have on our side to fight these *things*, and probably more who will fight with no heart or half a heart because in their own hearts they knew that this punishment was not right!' Pail drew his sword. 'But what I'm about to do is right!' he cried, slicing through the twine that bound the prisoners.

And no-one moved to stop him.

Later, when it was starting to get dark and people began to settle for the night, Venn went to check on Havoc who was lying in some straw just inside the compound. The horse's breathing was better now, less shallow and more regular, thanks to Father Mally who had also cleaned his wounds and made a poultice for some of the deeper cuts. After a few minutes, Venn heard a familiar step and turned.

'Hi, Dad,' he said.

'How's the nag?'

'He's not a ...' began Venn, feeling his temperature rise. He half-closed his eyes and breathed, 'he's fine, thanks. I really think he'll pull through.' Stirn, for his part, inwardly cursed himself – he'd always called horses *nags*, but his son's mount had nothing in common with the flea-ridden things that pulled the occasional cart about the village. He tried again.

'Speaks well, your friend.'

'Pail?'

'Aye, that's him. He speaks well, you fight well – I'll grant you that. And your cousin – Giff, well ... um,' Venn glanced up, already half smiling as he father scratched his head. '... 'e can certainly eat!' And the tension eased as they both smiled at each other. After some more reflection, Stirn even began to laugh quietly. "e ate half that pig on his own, y'know. I thought old Cobb was going to have a hernia!'

'He's improved, you should have seen him a couple of months ago – Pail kept calling him Sir Scoffalot!'

'Har, har!' Stirn sat down. 'That's a good one – Maisy'll love it – Sir *Scoffalot* – don't tell your Aunt Didee, though – you know how protective of her little darling she is!'

Venn shook his head; he turned to stroke Havoc who tried to look up to see what all the noise was about. When he turned back, he wasn't surprised to see his father looking serious again. 'What is it, Dad?'

Stirn looked at the floor. 'Bane and that other one – the mad thing, Squawk – they'll be back … maybe not tomorrow. But the next day is my guess. Look, son, you did well today … but you got lucky …'

'But …!'

'… but nothing – *you* got lucky. And Bane, well, he won't mess about. We ain't seen what he can do yet but I reckon he's got it in 'im to slaughter the lot of us and not give a rat's tail about it. You've got to go tomorrow … if not for your sake, then ours. They'll punish us, but without that Bludge, things might get easier now … the others, they may have celebrated today but have you noticed, they're all back in the compound tonight.'

Venn felt his fists ball and tried to ride out a sudden rage, so strong that it made his head feel fuzzy. His father couldn't wait to belittle what he had done. He was probably jealous that he hadn't got rid of Bludge in seven years. His anger found its voice before he could stop himself. 'I CAN'T BELIEVE …!'

But his father was onto him, his own quick temper rising to meet Venn's. 'NEVER!' he bellowed back. 'NEVER RAISE YOUR VOICE TO ME IN THIS VILLAGE AGAIN! I AM STILL YOUR FATHER, OR HAVE YOU FORGOTTEN THAT, MR. HIGH AND MIGHTY?'

'*Father?*' Venn was properly angry now. 'You stopped being my father when you sent us away!' And the second he said it, he wished in his soul that he hadn't.

Something in his father's face seemed to dry up and die.

His jaw worked and Venn even thought he might strike him. He sort of hoped that he would, for he knew he deserved it. Venn looked at the once strong hands; the very same hands that had made things for him, played games with him, held onto him. They had been more familiar to him than his own but now he no longer recognised them, they looked so old. Old and weak. Eventually Stirn found his voice. It came out harsh – barely a whisper – but whether through anger or pain it was hard to tell.

'It would crush your mother, if she heard that ... thing is, son, I just don't think I know you anymore.'

But before Venn could reply, to say he was sorry, Pail came running in. He looked first at Stirn, then at Venn, his intelligent eyes reading the tension between them. 'Sorry,' he said, 'but I've just been outside the compound. It's Bludge.'

'What about him?' Venn was already up, suddenly relieved to have an excuse to get away.

'He's gone.'

CHAPTER 10
Giff's Adventure

For the first time in weeks, when Giff opened his eyes, the sun was already well over the trees. It was late. His waking thought was that the cider must have been stronger than it tasted, and so, feeling thick-headed and sleepy, he tottered out of the barn where he'd spent the night. The first person he clapped eyes on was Soozie. 'Yoo hoo!' she called, coming over from across the courtyard. 'Mornin', *Sire*,' she grinned, dropping a cheeky curtsey and winking.

'Hi, Soozie,' replied Giff, trying to sound nonchalant. He moved to edge past her but she was a lot quicker than she looked.

'*Oooh*, I likes a man with straw in 'is locks,' she said, running her hand through Giff's hair. Any pretend coolness on Giff's part vanished in an instant.

'Me too,' squeaked Giff, then thought about what he'd just said. 'No! I mean, er, I don't like men … I like straw! … um, actually, I like neither … really.' If she was at all put off by his gibbering, she didn't seem to show it.

'Maybees you could show me where you found all that lurvely golden straw, all comfy and warm,' she simpered, winding the strand she'd pulled out of his hair around her finger.

'Of course!' Giff fairly shouted, not knowing if he meant it or if he didn't. He just felt he had to escape – right away. Then come back later. Perhaps when he'd got himself a bit more together. 'But first I've got to talk to Venn and Pail. Er, have you seen them, by any chance?'

Soozie pouted but nevertheless tilted her head in the

direction of the compound. 'They're in there. Bein' miserable.'

Sure enough, he found his friends in the compound courtyard having breakfast. Even though he wouldn't have exactly described himself as the most sensitive of people, Giff picked up on the atmosphere immediately. Pail's parents, Simon and June, had gone back to looking as if the sun was about to turn to coal, whilst Venn and Stirn appeared to be having a scowling-intensely-into-their-porridge contest.

Pail, who had been scribbling things on bits of parchment, caught Giff's eye and shook his head quickly, as if to say, *don't say anything*. 'Bludge's carcass and head were taken late last night,' he whispered, coming over. 'Stirn wants to call a meeting to decide what to do.'

At this, Giff rolled his eyes, his good humour evaporated – not another bloody meeting where everyone shouts and then things get decided all in a rush at the end that please nobody. Giff made a snap decision. He had to get out. 'I'm going for a walk,' he said shortly and turned on his heel.

To avoid bumping into – well, anyone else – he nipped out of a small gate at the back of the stockade.

At least Soozie didn't go about the place looking like someone had peed in her broth. The problem with Pail and Venn – and roughly half the people in Four Frogs, now that Giff came to think about it – was that they could never look on the bright side; perhaps they just didn't want to. As he skirted the outside wall of the compound and headed into the woods he felt a huge weight lift from his shoulders. Things weren't all that bad. It was a lovely sunny day, they'd shown that they could defeat these Iron Knights – and that was just Venn! A minute or two more and he felt sure

Squawk would have been history.

As far as he was concerned, they were almost real knights; they had all the kit and yet they had hardly had a single bit of fun since this whole thing had started. And it *was* a lovely sunny day. Quite frankly, he might as well have stayed at Locke Castle.

So Giff strode out into the mid-morning sun, determined to do something interesting and have some fun at the same time.

♣

At first, he wandered somewhat aimlessly, retracing old steps from his early childhood when he spent most of his spare time with Pail and Venn in the woods, following familiar pathways and tracks until he felt like he was reliving an old dream. He cut himself a switch of ash and whistled as he walked, absentmindedly slicing the head off nettles he passed, remembering a different time, before all this started. Then, gradually, without really being aware of it, his feet took him in a more deliberate direction.

He headed north.

By the time Rainbeard's Castle came into view, he had made up his mind to go inside. He felt that reckless.

♣

Giff pushed his way through the thick undergrowth that hung across the secret path – the one that they had taken all those years ago, leading to the stone arch with its strange canal system. The water still went both ways, although, judging by the strange gurgling noises, he guessed it was being pumped from somewhere and that there was no magic involved. Makes sense though, he thought – Locke Castle had its own well, but it also relied heavily on a small army of water-carriers to lug buckets of water up from the river every morning. A continual supply of fresh water being pumped into the Castle would save people a lot of time, not to mention bad backs. The well was really just for witches and emergencies.

He paused at the stone arch, but failed to notice how the grass around it seemed to have been flattened recently. Instead, he pressed on to the curtain wall. Arriving there, he looked up at the crumbling battlements, searching for any signs of the Knights, but when no black visors appeared over the stone walls he spat on his hands and began to climb.

By the time he got to the top, he was panting, partly because he was carrying a sword and wearing a mail shirt but also, he had to admit, because he was out of practice. It was funny how the older you got, the less you wanted to climb up things.

Giff drew his sword and looked around. What struck him most was the silence. A gentle breeze blew a few leaves across the empty courtyard and the remains of the rotten staircase creaked like the dry timbers of a beached ship.

It was surprising how little it had changed. You'd have thought with all their clanking on about work, power, service, the Iron Knights might have tidied up once in a while.

Giff moved across the stone flags, keeping a wary eye on the huge door. At the slightest sign of the Iron Knights he planned to throw pride out of the window (and perhaps himself, if it came to it) and scarper. Not wearing full armour, he was fairly sure he could outrun them but it would be good to start with a nice lead.

So he tiptoed across the courtyard, only realising how stupid he must have looked when he got to the other side and had reached the main entrance.

The large oak door still hung on its hinges, leaves still gathered about the steps. Everything was *still* still. It might as well have been as if time up at the Castle had gradually slowed to a crawl and then stopped altogether. He peered inside.

But something in here wasn't right. The mirror had gone.

But that wasn't everything; the atmosphere inside was oppressive, as if something terrible had just happened, or was about to happen. Shadows were somehow starker, darker and they fell at odd angles to each other, as if the actual light coming through the tall, thin windows made no difference to how the shadows formed.

This is more like it, thought Giff. He was on an adventure.

And so he crept inside. Cowering down in the village, calling meetings, arguing amongst themselves. Whoever heard of a real knight being on a *committee*. He was taking the fight to the Iron Knights, to the seat of the evil. Surprise was the best form of defence, and they'd never be expecting him to actually go to the castle.

Listening for any noise, he crept up the long staircase, his hand on the hilt of his sword, ready to draw it in an instant. Reaching the long corridor, he was glad that they had memorised the stones that sat on springs – the ones that made the claws spring out and grab trespassers. Gingerly, he sidestepped around each booby trap and eventually made it to the hallway at the end of which was the Fast Tower and the Harp Staircase. And all the time, the pressure built; the dust-deadened silence, the strange, cheerless atmosphere and the terrible expectation that he could be caught at any moment built to a pitch.

He hadn't been sure about this foray when he had been climbing up the curtain wall, but now, as he looked up at the huge staircase with its musical wires twisting its way to the doorway at the top, almost out of view, he knew he had to get all the way up there. Giff was going back to the room where it all started.

Going over to the window, he looked out of it and noticed, with some satisfaction, that his hunch had been right. The exterior wooden staircase that had collapsed had originally been secured to the side of the building with a series of iron hinges that, though rusty and twisted, still studded the wall of the tower at roughly three-foot intervals, all the way to the top. If he was careful, he could get to Rainbeard's old study without using the musical staircase that would give him away.

Giff began to climb once more.

He had to admit, being outside and back in the sunlight was a relief after the oppressive feeling inside the Castle, and he enjoyed the exercise with the sun in his face.

Then he made the mistake of looking down. Giff froze.

A couple of minutes later, he stopped staring at the stones two inches from his nose as if his life depended on it and forced his grip on the metal hinge to relax. If I was only three feet off the ground, he told himself, then this would be easy – it's all in the mind. I'm not going to fall just because I'm a hundred and fifty feet up. A gentle wind stirred, it was cool and it dried the sweat on his forehead. Slowly, Giff's breathing began to return to normal and his heart stopped hammering. He plucked up his courage and resumed his climb.

Within a few minutes he had nearly reached Rainbeard's eyrie at the top of the Fast Tower and he was beginning to enjoy himself again. Coming to the first window, the old staircase had left a few rotten planks under the sill, like a small platform. Avoiding these, he grasped the stonework and peered inside as carefully as he could. He couldn't see anything except the long table that appeared to be even dustier than when he had last been there seven years ago, and the Viewing Tube that made everything look bigger.

This looked like it had been used recently because it was the only clean thing in the room and angled towards the village. They've been using this to spy on us, Giff realised. Suddenly, he had a purpose other than just snooping about.

He had another look around to make sure the room was empty, then hoisted himself through the window and dropped down, his soft shoes only making the slightest scuffing noise.

Just then, something at the extreme edge of his peripheral vision moved. A book fell off the table next to his head as a small but crystal clear voice in Giff's head said, *Uh, oh.*

Still crouching – hardly daring to breathe – Giff steeled himself and, ever so slowly, he turned his head.

Even so, when he looked around, he nearly cried out in horror as he saw the towering shape of Bane slowly unbend, stand and look around. Giff was so close he could have reached out and touched the Iron Knight. Every hair on his body, every goose bump and every bone suddenly felt like it had a cold electrical current running through it. *Run!* Screamed the small voice.

As luck would have it, but just for the moment, Giff was invisible to Bane because the small table Bane had been sitting at shielded him as did a small screen – the one that had prevented Giff from seeing the Iron Knight when he first looked in. However, the moment Bane moved forward, even by half a foot, the boy would be seen.

Without thinking, Giff slipped the fallen book inside his shirt just as Bane moved.

It was now or never.

Springing up, Giff dashed across the room. Bane turned and uttered a low growl as Giff picked up the Viewing Tube in both hands and hurled it out of the window with a huge effort. Then, without pausing, he followed it.

Bane's iron hand made a grab for him, almost, but not quite, snagging his belt as Giff went head first over the ledge and into the void.

He fell.

Actually, he was fervently hoping that one of the metal hinges was within reach. This was one time that he needed a bit of luck.

Fortunately, he got some.

As he went flying over the ledge, trying to ignore the huge drop all the way down to the flagstones where Rainbeard's Viewing Tube lay twisted and smashed, he saw a metal bracket sticking out, just within reach. Giff grabbed it with one hand, his dive suddenly changing direction from straight down the outside of the Fast Tower to a certain death, to something resembling an acrobat's loop. His speed stopped dead and his arm felt as if it was about to be torn from his collarbone. But the metal held and so did his grip. Just.

As he looked around for the next iron bolt, he saw Bane's malevolent iron mask with the pinpricks of red light stare down at him and then disappear back inside. He would surely be taking the stairs now, to meet him at the bottom.

Giff climbed so fast down the remains of the old staircase, it was really just controlled falling. He had to jump the last eight feet or so and hit the ground more heavily than he would have liked. He leapt up and began to run. About halfway across the courtyard, he risked turning around and saw, to his horror, Bane was now striding out of the door towards him, sword drawn, moving with purpose.

Giff immediately found a turn of speed he never knew he

had; reaching the curtain wall in seconds, he leapt over the balustrade and dropped several feet before using the creepers to break his fall. At least my climbing's getting better, he thought as he reached the ground and ran for the safety of the wood.

He was in such a hurry that he ran through a tall patch of stinging nettles, tripped over several rabbit holes and nearly lost his sword in some brambles before he finally burst onto the path, more by luck than judgement.

Ha ha! He congratulated himself; I'm safe, I broke into the Castle, smashed the Viewing Tube, so they can't spy on us anymore, got away from Bane – just wait until I tell the others! And he sped along the track, away from the Castle, past the waterways, under the arch … and right into the path of Squawk.

Chapter 11
~: *Squawk* :~

As he tried desperately to stop before he crashed into the second Iron Knight he had bumped into that morning, and draw his sword all at the same time, Giff was forced to admit that it had been an especially bad day for meeting the wrong people. For his part, Squawk hadn't shown any signs of having noticed the unexpected company in his leafy glade beneath the arch.

For the moment, he seemed to be entirely engrossed in what he was doing, which was walking around in stiffed-legged circles. Once in a while, he would utter a strange 'DAK!' sound and hop in the air – the effect making him look all the more like a distracted cockerel.

The gaping rent in his helmet that Giff had made with his sword still emitted a small fountain of sparks every so often. If there had been any dry hay or grass nearby it would probably have caught fire.

I could turn and run now, said Giff to himself – but what with Soozie, his friends and their meeting, and then the recent encounter with the malevolent Bane, Giff decided there and then that he had had enough of avoiding things for one day. Squawk may have been over two foot taller than him, fully armed and dangerously insane, but Giff still felt that he could beat him – even if he only wore a mail shirt and carried no shield.

'Knight!' At Giff's cry, Squawk uttered a yelp of surprise, skipped and turned at the same time.

'DAK!' he grated and jabbed his lance in the air angrily. 'DAK, DAK, DAK, ADAK, ADAAK!'

Giff stepped forward, into the centre of the circle, draw

his sword back with one hand, and beckoned with the other. 'Yes, attack … be my guest! Let's finish what we started.'

'ADAAK, ADAAK, ADAAAAK!' the cogs and wheels inside Squawk's metal torso wound to a high-pitched scream as he ran around and around in a mad, tight circle, then sling-shot out of his own trajectory straight at Giff.

As he charged the boy, Squawk kept the point of his spear high, only at the very last instant moving it low to jab at Giff's exposed legs. It was then that Giff noticed that the lance had serrated edges on one edge, like a pike's teeth. A cut from that would be impossible to stitch and would probably get infected.

Giff, who had very little practice fighting opponents with spears, was very nearly fooled by the move but managed to sidestep just in time. As Squawk cantered past him, Giff struck, the flat of his blade catching Squawk on the back of the head. There was a huge, hollow ringing sound and Squawk turned, his whole head now vibrating like a gong.

'**adaaaaaak!**' he cried again, flapping his arms. Something must have been wrong with his coordination; when his right arm went up, his left leg shot out at an angle and seemed to stick there. Squawk tottered and would have fallen over had he not used his lance as a hasty crutch.

The vibration slowly faded and Squawk's coordination returned.

He charged at Giff again, missing by a few feet as he carried on past the boy and into the base of a tree. One of the spikes on his armour got embedded in the trunk and he was stuck fast for a few moments.

Before Giff had a chance to take advantage of the opportunity and finish him off with his sword, Squawk managed to wrench himself free and turn.

Next, the Iron Knight tried a series of erratic but very rapid jabs. Some were mere feints, to draw Giff out; others were probing, forcing Giff to defend himself. It took a few moments to work out what Squawk was up to, but he quickly realised that the feints were the most dangerous attack of all. Squawk was trying to make Giff lunge too far forward, at which point he would make a grab for the boy's sword. This gave Giff an idea.

After two or three more feints that Giff made a great show of being confused and frightened by, he went into retreat, pretending to trip and stumble. Squawk, sensing a possible victory, got very excited and over-extended one of his own thrusts.

Giff saw his chance – it might be the only one he got. As Squawk thrust the serrated point at him again, aiming to gut the boy, Giff dropped his guard fractionally. This allowed the vicious point of the lance to pass by his own blade, whereupon it would surely have continued on through Giff's mail shirt and into the soft tissue of his stomach, but for the blade-catcher that wound in thick bands about the hilt of Giff's sword, an addition by Venn.

The lance slotted into the mesh and was trapped in the hilt of Giff's sword, its jagged edge making it impossible to draw out again. Squawk uttered a yip of annoyance and tried to give it a tug – strong enough that it would have surely pulled Giff off his feet. But Giff was too fast and he knew what he was going to do. Before Squawk could attempt anything, he twisted his arm and wrist. He felt the mesh lock Squawk's blade; with all his strength, he heaved. There was a grinding noise and Giff felt huge resistance. Just when he thought nothing would happen, he felt the blade snap.

Squawk gave an almighty tug at that very moment but, with the spear's blade broken, there was no longer anything holding it in place. Squawk, who was already off balance, stumbled backwards and fell.

'AARK?!' he cried as he lay on his back, looking at the broken end of his weapon – his beaked, blank visor somehow conveyed his surprise and horror. He had very little time to reflect on his misfortune as Giff pressed his advantage.

'Ha!' Giff cried, swinging his sword and lopped another two feet off the lance. Squawk raised the remains of his weapon to defend himself as he deftly struck again, but this time the lance splintered and Giff felt his sword strike home. The sheer effort had made him close his eyes briefly, but when he opened them again, he saw that he had sliced off his opponent's iron hand, just above the wrist. There was a shower of sparks from the severed limb. This was it.

Giff took his broadsword in both hands, raising it above his head, intending to bring it down on the Iron Knight's neck.

Squawk could do nothing as he watched the blade rise, ready to fall on him in a deathblow, but then his gaze continued to travel upwards as a broad shadow materialised across the trampled grass. Something wasn't right. Some early instinct, born of ancestors who lived in dark caves, made Giff turn.

The charred remains of Bludge towered up behind him. Blackened iron arms, heat-distorted and twisted, swung the melted remains of his mace. His head had been fixed on but at an alarming angle so that a huge gap between his shoulder and neck gave vent to the hollow furnace of rage from within.

Giff took one look at the monster and legged it.

Chapter 12
~: *Siege* :~

Barely a week later and Four Frogs was back to being a hellhole. Worse than before: Re-broken cottages, smashed fences and the forlorn carcasses of sheep lay scattered in the mud that had been churned over by the incessant patrolling of the Iron Knights who now laid siege to the compound.

And Venn was sick.

He lay on a low bunk and sweated with a raging fever that had sprung up from nowhere the day that Giff went to the Castle. His father never left his bedside, even when he started to look ill himself – a combination of exhaustion, lack of food and years of concern had begun to take their toll on a once strong man. His wife eventually took matters in hand and forced Stirn to go to bed, promising she would stay by their son at all times.

Trapped inside their wooden stockade, the villagers dared not attempt an escape. Without Venn to lead them, the Iron Knights had once more gained the upper hand.

Pail, for his part, seemed lost in his own thoughts, morose and depressed. He spent his days looking through the driving rain, out at the Iron Knights. Someone observing him closely would have noticed how he shuddered each time the thin form of Bane swept into view. Giff was at a complete loss of what to do.

The only bright side, if one could call it that, was the fact that everyone seemed to be working together – for the time being, at least. Instead of family groups huddling together, as they had done when Venn, Pail and Giff had first arrived, Four Frogs had rallied; now, they all shared the dwindling supply of food and water evenly amongst everyone: children first, followed by the old, the sick and the most needy. Even Pittle and Brother Pike seemed to be included and received their daily ration the same as everyone else.

Honour, friendship and loyalty was working.

It was what Pail had been talking about when Giff had burst in, straight from his encounter with Bludge.

❧

'*Honos, amicitia, fides!* We might not be knights but the message to us is clear! Without each other, without support from everyone, we're dead …!' He stopped talking and turned around as Giff came through the door. 'What's wrong with you?' he asked, looking testy, 'you look like you've seen a ghost.'

Breathing heavily, Giff collapsed in a heap on the rough earth floor of the meeting room, as Soozie jumped forward to help him. He had run so fast through the woods, he had almost no recollection of how he had got back to Four Frogs. The thought of Bludge's coal-blackened armour had kept him sprinting like a duck across water until he got inside the relative safety of the walls. He still had the heebeejeebies. And he was definitely going to have nightmares. 'Yeah, you might say that,' he gasped as Soozie mopped his head with a hanky. 'Been up at the Castle … Bludge is alive and well – bit crispy, but he's as mad as a bucket full of frogs.'

'You did *what!*' Pail looked furious, as did many of the villagers. Even his dad looked a bit upset.

'Look, I got this!' Giff said quickly – it had been a bad enough day without getting lynched by a baying mob of angry villagers – and he fished inside his shirt and pulled out a lump of the smashed spying tube that he had picked up from the flagstones at the foot of the Fast Tower. 'They won't be able to see what we're up to now – not without coming down.' He looked around with some satisfaction at the slightly mollified faces around him. 'And I also pinched this – it's for you, Pail,' he said, handing him a slim black volume. 'Bane was reading it, so it might be important.'

'You *saw* Bane?' Giff looked up and noticed Venn for the first time. His fever must have already begun to take hold because his skin was slick with sweat and he had gone the colour of skimmed milk.

'Yup,' Giff confirmed and proceeded to tell them everything that had happened.

After he had finished, there was complete silence before Stirn nodded slowly. 'Well, boy, I suppose, on balance, you did well. But you could have got yerself sliced in half by Bane or crushed by Bludge. Squawk's nearly done in, you say? I suppose that's something, too.

'Now, we've heard a lot of talk whilst you've been gone and thanks to you, we've got a bit more information to go on. I was right; they'll definitely be back now … I'd say tomorrow. So tonight, we don't sleep. Every man, woman and child who is old enough to help is going out in groups to cut more wood to add to the walls. We need thickness and height. Those that are too young or too ill to work can keep a look out!'

※

And so they worked all night; slowly, hour by hour, the wall got higher as bigger wooden stakes cut down from trees in the woods were added. Just as muted birdsong signalled the arrival of dawn, there was a shout from Father Mally, stationed up the road. The Iron Knights were coming. All three. Men, women and children dropped what they were carrying and ran.

Venn hardly made it into the compound before he collapsed.

♣

That had been six days ago and now the food was running out. They had enough water remaining for two days – if the adults went without, three.

No-one was saying anything, but as Giff looked around at the grim fathers, the mothers, hollow-eyed and fearful, and the thin children, he knew many villagers must be close to breaking. It would take only one mother to panic when her child fell ill, to desperately ask for more food, or to simply take it; and the combination of fear, hunger and the sense of being trapped could spill over into civil war.

Venn, who had become a symbol of strength and hope after he had beaten Bludge, had become a ghost of himself. There were real fears he might get worse. His breathing mirrored Havoc's, who was slowly recovering against everyone's expectations, but who still lay in the corner. Venn was no longer the reassuring presence, the bedrock on which to base their hopes and calm the fears that the iron monsters would eventually decide to break in.

Actually Giff had been wondering about that. Why did the Knights not simply smash the walls down and storm the compound in one merciless bout of fury? Since they had come down from the castle, something had held Bane back. It was almost as if he, too, was fearful of something.

Instead of storming the compound then, they kept up a ceaseless tramping around the walls, day and night: Bane, a silent stalking presence; Bludge, charred – alternately bellowing and howling, as if still tortured by flames; and Squawk, jerking about like a mad puppet, now properly insane. It was he who had killed all the sheep.

And all the time their continual grating and clanking as they marched in ceaseless circles around the wooden walls, keeping the terrified children awake through the long nights.

⚜

'We have to do something,' said Giff on the seventh evening. Pail looked up from his reading. His eyes seemed unfocused and Giff suddenly realised something – he hadn't seen his friend without the black book in his hand since the evening he gave it to him. 'Does it say anything useful?' he asked casually, pointing at the dark volume. Pail jumped like he'd been pinched and immediately put the book in his pocket. It was as if he didn't want Giff to so much as look at the cover.

'No, not really,' his voice was strained. 'It's just …' he paused, '… it's a little hard to understand, that's all.' Pail re-focused. 'What do you suppose we can do?'

Giff knew he wasn't exactly the best person at coming up with ideas but he would have thought the answer was obvious. 'We have to go out and fight them.'

'Without Venn, we'd lose,' said Pail simply.

Giff shook his head vigorously. 'I don't think so. Squawk can't fight and I don't think even Bludge can move properly anymore.'

'But Bane,' Pail's face darkened. 'He will kill us all, the moment the gate opens.'

'I don't think so!' Giff was getting frustrated, 'he's scared, or something's making him hesitate … it must be, otherwise he would have come in by now.'

Pail half closed his eyes and turned to face the window where the rain still poured down in the dusk. Three figures could be seen through the driving wet. 'He's waiting for us to run out of food, to start fighting amongst ourselves. To weaken ourselves from within – classic siege tactics.'

'Very neat,' Giff scoffed, 'but you don't believe that anymore than I do. There's something else going on, I can feel it.'

'You do not know the ways of Bane.'

'Oh, and I suppose you do. I suppose it's all in that book of yours!'

Pail's head snapped up and he gave his friend a piercing stare. Giff knew he'd hit a nerve. This was it, the argument that had been brewing for days was about to erupt. Pail opened his mouth, but before the words came out there was a small commotion over in the corner of the dormitory where Havoc lay. Both boys turned.

'– 'e's getting up!' said Mistress Moon, jumping about excitedly. 'I nevir thought I'd see that hoss on 'is four legs agin.' And sure enough, with a series of snorts, Havoc had righted himself. He gave a determined shake of his mane, and, after a couple of false starts, he forced himself onto his front feet first, and then, with a massive effort, onto his back legs.

'Give 'im some space!'

Havoc stood, wobbled there for a few moments, his front legs locked but his hindquarters swaying slightly. His huge muscles bunched under his gleaming black hide, as if he was testing his strength, and he gave another snort of satisfaction.

At the other end of the compound, Knobble and Socrates must have heard him because they whinnied from their stables in reply. Havoc raised his head and his nostrils flared.

Then, picking carefully through the beds, past the villagers who fell back to make way for him, he trod a meandering path slowly across the dormitory to where Venn lay. Once he got there, Havoc's large brown eyes considered his master for a few moments, before, slowly and very gently, he stretched his head down and gently nuzzled Venn, making a curious nickering noise in the back of his throat as he did so.

Venn eyelids fluttered half-open. He eyes focused.

'Hello, my horse,' he said with a weak smile. He blinked and then looked around at the faces of the people crowding around his cot. Venn smiled wanly again. 'The fever's passing, I think,' he said and closed his eyes.

CHAPTER 13
~: *The Last Battle* :~

PAIL WAS UP before anybody else. Wrapping the bed covers around his hunched shoulders, he slipped as silently as he could past the rows of people sleeping on the floor and left the dormitory. Once outside, in the compound, he stole across its small courtyard and took up station by the eyehole that had been cut in the timber.

For a moment, the village square beyond the stockade looked empty. In the half-light of dawn, Pail couldn't stop himself from hoping that the siege was over. But just a few seconds later Bane came into view – a creeping, malign presence that stalked the walls relentlessly.

Then Bludge appeared from nowhere, appearing so un-expectedly close to the stockade that Pail panicked and jumped backwards with a cry, reaching for a sword that wasn't there. Bane made a growling noise deep in his throat, and the other Iron Knight reluctantly drew back from the walls that he could so easily have smashed to kindling.

Anyone else seeing this exchange would have been puzzled, but Pail knew exactly what had occurred and, more to the point, he knew what he had to do about it. It was all in the book – Giff was right about that. But Pail had also been telling the truth when he stated that Bane's plan was to weaken them – perhaps even to the point of death – or let civil war break out.

He heard a step behind him and turned. Venn stood there, looking somewhat drawn but otherwise much better. His mail shirt was already on and he was buckling his heavy sword belt around his waist. His face was set – grim, even – making him look much older than his fifteen years. 'We've got to do something. It won't be long before one of the children gets really sick and someone makes a break for it.'

'And when they do, those creatures out there will cut them down one by one. It's what It wants,' agreed Pail, referring to Bane.

Venn caught something in Pail's voice. 'Are you alright?'

'Yeah, fine,' lied Pail, 'but what about you?'

'I've felt better,' Venn grinned, 'but what choice do we have?'

'Damn straight! Blimey, you two look like crap.' Giff was up too, fully armed and absurdly cheerful. They looked at each other. Pail sniffed.

'Let's finish this thing,' said Venn.

***

So they went out.

It had taken them a while to put the remainder of their armour on, but they had to dress with care, to make sure nothing came undone and fell off during battle and that none of their plate armour was lose enough to let a sword slide through a gap and maim.

Pail finished by strapping Frobisher's giant broadsword around his waist and pulled on his heavy leather gauntlets, ribbed with iron, that would protect the backs of his hands from a deep slice. His helm felt somewhat tight and restricting but, as they stepped out of the compound and into full view of the Iron Knights, he glanced left. Pail noticed how the bright red plumes on Venn's helm caught the breeze and how the early rising sun shone off Giff's breastplate and, at that moment, he just knew that the three of them looked bloody impressive. By anyone's standards.

They opened the stockade gate and stepped out.

As soon as Bludge spotted the three boys, he turned and

howled in anger and in expectation; the noise brought Squawk from the edge of the wood, covered in mud and still fizzling.

Initially, Pail thought the Iron Knights would charge, but, as Bludge went to move forward, Bane drew his long thin sword and banged it forcefully on Bludge's breastplate, forcing him to hold back. Squawk, suddenly realising that he was alone, stopped halfway to the boys, gave one of his little jumps and zig-zagged back to the other two.

'See,' said Giff, 'they're way more scared of us than we are of them. Like spiders!'

'How many seven foot spiders made of solid iron do you know?' asked Pail.

'Well, at least they've learned to fear us,' said Venn, ' so they're holding back – it's up to us to take the fight to them.'

'I'll take Bane,' said Pail.

'You what?' Up until now, Giff had assumed Venn, as the strongest amongst them, would take on Bane. So had Venn.

'No,' he said, 'he'll kill you in an instant.' Pail had got his stubborn face on. Both Giff and Venn knew it was hopeless – from their earliest childhood they had learned that expression and what it meant. Making Pail see sense was like knitting fog when he looked like that.

'You're still weak,' explained Pail, sounding reasonable. 'I'll hold It off – I've got the longest reach. That way you two can deal with Bludge and Squawk. It's our only hope. With those two out of the way, we might just be able to defeat Bane together.' And even as he said it, he knew it wasn't true. But the other two seemed convinced enough to let it go. Bane was still utterly unknown as an opponent in battle. What was the point of worrying now? They just had to get on with it, thought Pail.

'Alright,' said Venn, 'keep your shields up as you go in, and tight against mine. Watch for Squawk; even with one hand, he'll try and use what's left of that lance of his to jab our legs or prise our shields apart. But keep close to them, however much you don't want to. It'll stop Bludge getting a proper swing at us.' Venn turned and stared across at their opponents, drawing his sword.

'You!' he shouted, pointing his blade directly at Bane's heart. 'Today, you creatures die. Before sundown, we will destroy you. Your body parts will be used to mend our walls and your heads will be weighted with stones and thrown in our deepest lakes. Your ruby hearts will be traded for cattle, sheep and corn to replace what you have destroyed, and by the morning you will be no more than a despised memory. I tell you this, for I am Venn, *I am a warrior and I will destroy you!*'

'Not bad,' muttered Giff.

'Thanks, I thought so, too.' Then Venn looked either side of him before pulling his shield up. 'Let's go, boys!'

As they went forward, all three felt a wave of fear, in spite of the adrenalin that was pumping through their bodies. The Knights were huge, dwarfing even Venn, their massive metal arms clanking, insides whirring as their feet stamped the ground, making it shake.

When they got within ten feet, the Iron Knights stopped stamping. They put their shields up, forming their own short shield wall. This was going to be hard. The words *work, power, service* were emblazoned on the Iron Knights' shields, set against a black circle; it was a stark contrast to the plain shields the boys carried, which served to remind Pail that they were not knights. Real knights would have their own coat of arms and motto.

Bludge's first two blows landed on Venn's shield, buckling it. Venn's arm went numb. But the third blow, when it came, just glanced off – they were now too close, as Venn had predicted, and Bludge was unable to get a proper swing.

Milliseconds later, the tremendous crash of six shields colliding woke those villagers not already stirring in their bunks.

From the start, Squawk was only just holding rank. Wholly over-excited, he was hopping up and down, one-armed, waving his broken spear in the air. 'Dak, dak, ada'aak!' Giff, ignoring the way his helmet was rubbing painfully against his jaw, jinked his head to avoid the lance. Then, seeing his chance, he took a swing at Squawk's head.

From nowhere, Bane's sword shot across their ranks and blocked the blow. Pail tried to strike out at Bane and although he caught the top of Bane's forearm, he barely made a scratch. Pail struck out again but Bane moved like lightning and parried his thrust so harshly that Pail almost dropped his sword.

Soon, it became more of a shoving match than anything else. The boys pushed with all their might, trying to get the shield wall in front of them to break; the Iron Knights held their ground, Bludge or Squawk occasionally having a go at crushing or spearing the boys in front of them, but they mainly seemed content to defend.

It took Pail a while to realise it but, in fact, Bane was simply using the same tactics he had employed in the siege. He was waiting until his opponents destroyed themselves.

To Stirn and the others watching from the stockade, it looked as if Venn, Pail and Giff were doing well but bit by bit, the adrenalin was wearing off. Venn, who was still running a slight fever, suddenly felt immensely tired. His arms were heavy, making it more difficult by the minute to hold his shield up. They had been fighting hard, pushing forwards and fending off blows for over ten minutes. They were holding their own, but making no real progress and, as yet, Bane had hardly been involved.

'Come on!' Pail yelled through his visor, his teeth gritted, 'fight me, you cowardly lump of pig iron!' But Bane was unmoved, casually brushing aside Pail's thrusts, keeping his shield locked with Squawk's on his left and Bludge's to his right. He was the lynchpin. If they couldn't move him, Venn and Giff would not be able to reach Squawk or Bludge. Giff was tiring too, and his shield kept dipping dangerously low. He hadn't eaten properly in a week and his mouth felt parched, like it was full of dry ash.

Venn saw what Pail knew all too clearly. They would slowly get more and more tired until their shields dropped and the death blow, when it came from Bludge's molten mace or Squawk's hastily repaired lance, would hardly be noticed through their exhaustion.

So, this was it, Venn thought. He was filled with a sudden sense of infinite sadness, well beyond his years. What had seemed so heroic a few minutes ago suddenly seemed childish and futile. They had left the stockade, hoping to force the Iron Knights into one last charge, a furious quick battle that could decide all of their fates in a few lucky blows. Instead, they were to get this: pushing forward like toy soldiers against these massive lumps of forged metal, wires and cold steel. Finally, as the villagers watched their last hopes slowly fade, Bane would strike and it would all be over – for them, for their families and for the rest of of Four Frogs. It was entirely their fault. In spite of all the years of hard training, Venn felt like crying.

Coldly sensing that their moment had come, Bludge raised the twisted remains of his great mace, Bane levelled his sword and Squawk stepped back the better to thrust. It would soon be over.

But the final blows never came.

CHAPTER 14

~: *Here comes the Cavalry* :~

ALL THREE IRON KNIGHTS seemed to freeze in mid-movement.

Their hearing must have been very acute, because it took Pail a few seconds to determine what it was that had caused them to stop dead virtually mid-swing.

Hooves. The sweet thunder of hooves.

He turned just in time to jump backwards as Frobisher's stallion – Riot, decked in full livery – tore through the Iron Knight's shield wall, temporarily making a gap appear in the ranks.

Bane was knocked sideways, but he rallied immediately and stepped forward to close the breach. Sir Godfrey on Clover came through, hot on his heels, forcing Bane back another step. And then it was Percival Locke whose lance splintered on Bane's breastplate.

'Ha, ha!' cried Percival, 'Just like old times!'

'I may be going senile,' said Frobisher, his voice sounding tinny inside a battered looking helmet, 'but I cannot, for the life of me, remember having to fight three giant mechanical knights in the middle of a quiet village in England when I was twenty.'

What the older knights had achieved with their charge didn't seem much but it was just enough for Giff to take advantage of the break in the action. He threw his shield to one side, raised his broadsword with both hands and, jumping in the air with a loud cry, brought it down on Squawk's already damaged head.

The spiked armour seemed to split in a shower of sparks and the blow triggered a drawn out '*Squaaaark!*' from Squawk. Giff felt a huge jolt run down his sword and through his armour, like nothing he could describe, and he was thrown backwards. When he looked up, the two neatly severed halves split and fell where they writhed on the grass.

'And that's what happens if you chase sheep!' he cried.

With twin roars, Bludge and Bane swung their shields round to close ranks but Venn was too quick for Bludge, who was slow, his charred joints and gears grating horribly. Before the Iron Knight could take a proper defensive stance, Venn chopped at Bludge's exposed forearm, hacking the metal limb off at the elbow.

Venn should have stepped away but he sensed victory. He came forward, his sword now scything upwards, making contact with the exposed workings under Bludge's chin, slicing through the hastily repaired wires and pulleys.

This may have all but severed the Knight's head for a second time had it not been for Bludge's arm, which was still scything around, aiming low under Venn's shield.

Luckily for Venn, Bludge had less strength than before and, as Giff remarked later, not having much of his head left probably didn't help. Nonetheless, the final blow of his mace made contact and smashed into Venn's leg, just below the knee. There was a horrible snapping noise and Venn cried out as he felt the whole of his leg give way.

❧

Seeing Venn fall, the villagers surged forward in anger. This forced Pail, Giff and Venn temporarily out of the way, forming a protective barrier around them, and effectively hemming Bane in – his back pressed against a large oak. Wielding axes normally used for chopping wood, cleavers for jointing meat, hay-forks and staves, they trampled over the broken hulks of Bludge and Squawk, right into the path of Bane's deadly sword.

By now Frobisher, Godfrey and Percival had wheeled around, orchestrating the concerted attack on the last remaining but most dangerous Iron Knight of all.

And it was then that they finally saw what he was capable of.

Within seconds, several of the villagers were grievously hurt as Bane's sword hummed in the air, a blur that sliced through the farm implements as if they were toys.

Like a snake, Bane glided forward, the back of his mailed fist slapping Brother Pike. The sheer force of the blow lifted him into the air and threw him several metres back. Farn took a similar blow to his cheek, knocking him out cold and he would have been crushed were it not for the quick thinking of Stirn, who grabbed and pulled him out of the way just as Bane's great metal foot came crashing down where his head had been moments before. The semi-circle around Bane widened as the villagers backed off.

Seeing that they were losing their advantage in numbers, Pail's father ran forward with a cry, jabbing a rusty pitchfork at Bane's torso. Bane's razor sharp sword flicked upwards and a crimson butterfly of blood immediately appeared on Simon's shirt. The poor man fell without a sound and Pail shot forward in dismay and fury.

'Dad!' he hefted his sword again. 'Move!' he yelled at the villagers who were blocking his path to Bane. 'He's mine! I'll take him alone!' Simon, bleeding heavily, managed to pull himself away from the fight.

Giff grabbed Pail's arm, holding him back. 'Have you gone bonkers?' Pail tried to shake Giff off but he was holding on too tight, so he was forced to stop and look at his friend, his dark eyes the only visible part of his face through the narrow vents in his visor.

'No, you don't understand … you were right, Giff, it really was all in the book you stole – Bane wasn't attacking because he knew I knew the secret, because I now had the book. If I die, then he dies. It's my blood. Don't you see – he used my blood! The book was clear about that. The other two are just mechanical automatons, like those clockwork birds that old Terence used to make for us. But Bane – he's different somehow, really dangerous. He can't be stopped with swords, spears or lances. This is the only way.'

'Excuse me for pointing out the bleeding obvious, but you'll die.'

'Thanks, Giff, yeah, I know, but I've been doing a lot of thinking over the last few days. It only dawned on me this morning when I got up and watched Bane patrolling the walls. Chivalry is like love – it's just another kind of giving. When our parents sent us away, they lost something that I don't think any of us will appreciate until we have kids of our own, but it nearly killed them.' Pail looked over at Bane, who seemed to be fighting at least fifteen people at once, including the three elderly knights on horseback, his arms moving in a blur. He seemed to be lost in his own world of mayhem and destruction.

The villagers rolled back from the onslaught, then rallied and surged forward like human waves retreating from and then returning to batter against some unstoppable barrier.

'Look, they're barely containing It, and when It breaks free, which It will do before long, then innocent people will start dying!'

This was his only chance; Pail knew that if he attacked Bane now, the Iron Knight would fight him through sheer elemental anger. He inspected the notched blade of his sword, then moved towards the fray; but as he did so, he turned to his friends. 'It's what being a knight is all about.

Anyone can do it, no matter where they were born. It's about giving. Real chivalry is sacrifice.'

'No!' shouted Venn desperately. 'I'll go!' But his leg was smashed – the only thing holding it straight was his armour – and he stumbled, his hand flaying, as Pail charged into his last battle.

Whether Pail was right and Bane was too far lost in his own tsunami of destructive force to notice that it was Pail, or whether he knew but was past caring, no-one could tell – least of all Bane himself, most probably. But, as Pail ran into the battle, aiming his long sword at Bane's stomach, Bane seemed to find another turn of speed. Stepping like a dancer to one side, he batted Pail's sword away with the edge of his shield. Then he skipped backwards half a pace and, straightening his arm, he brought the deadly point of his sword up to meet Pail who continued forward with a cry of 'BAAAANNNE!' that suddenly died on his lips.

Pail gasped but otherwise uttered no sound as he felt the unnaturally cold iron blade puncture the chain mail, slide past his ribs and slice through the soft tissue within.

He was even smiling softly, almost to himself, when Bane raised his sword, slowly lifting the boy off his feet.

As he bought Pail closer, the Iron Knight's visor clicked open, revealing the pitch-black workings and the iron skull within that might just as well have been carved from onyx. He seemed to be studying the boy, the red eyes, like twin coals, abruptly burning very bright. Something went click and his metal jaw moved open and closed a few times before any sound came out.

'Work,' he said, 'power … service,' the jaw clicked again, 'work, power, service, hate,' his arm began to shudder as if

Pail's weight was suddenly too much to bear, 'work, power, service, hate, die, weak, die, dead, nothing ... no Bane ... hate ... DIE!'

And then Bane's face started to melt, the iron inside blistering and bubbling, as if it was actually made of molten tar that began to run in gluts down his breastplate. Pail, still impaled and dying, coughed, bringing up his own flood of bright red blood in sharp contrast to the black ooze.

It's over, thought Giff: he had heard of warriors who said that no victory is ever complete, that there is always loss in any fight; and no battle wholly won, just less lost than the other side. Looking at the limp body of his friend, at the blood running from Pail down Bane's sword he suddenly knew what these old battle-scarred warriors had meant. This was the face of the friend he had seen every day of his childhood and today was the last day he would ever see it.

Bane's whole body seemed to erupt as his mangled insides gave an inhuman snarl. His iron skin welted as it peeled, like he was trying to turn himself inside out. Soon, he became a bubbling mass of evil-smelling pitch that writhed in paroxysms of agony and the villagers instinctively fell back in fear and disgust.

Finally, Bane's sword arm dropped and he sagged at his knees, his remains slowly toppling into the mud. Pail was at last released, sliding from the great blade where he dropped, lifelessly, onto the dirt.

The whole courtyard had gone deathly quiet as Pail's mother ran forward and fell to her knees beside her son with a cry that could only mean her heart was breaking.

CHAPTER 15
~: Visitor :~

Now, sometimes the world seems to revolve slowly, and events follow one another over a sedate period of quiet years. At other times, the revolutions quicken, and it is then that momentous occurrences come one right after another, with the speed of migrating swallows flashing across a late autumn sky. This was one such day.

With all that had been going on, it was hardly surprising that no-one noticed the third (and final) visitor to Four Frogs in recent times. This was an altogether unusual caller, even for the villagers, who justifiably felt that they had seen enough strangeness to last a lifetime. Both horse and rider were lightly clad in the same extraordinary ivory armour, the like of which no-one in England would ever have clapped eyes on. There was also something else about him …

❧

As the old knight approached the main square on his equally ancient and bony steed, he was oblivious to the mud, the broken houses and the grim stockade in the midst of what had once been a rather pretty square. His eye had long-since learned to dwell on that which was best in life and he was happily remarking to himself that Spring seemed well and truly sprung – meaning the delicate green shoots of bluebells were beginning to poke through the long grass by the roadside, the air seemed a little warmer than the day before, and the breeze fragrant with the delicate scent of early daffodils. Or perhaps he was just imagining that last bit. No matter either way. Now then …

'Why are you making all that noise, woman?' June looked up, as people fell back, tears streaking the dust on her face.

'It's my son, Sire. My only boy is dead.'

The old man studied Pail's corpse for a moment, as if giving all due seriousness to his mother's assertion.

'Nonsense!' he said, clambering off his horse with surprising energy. Although this statement was made firmly, there was a sort of gentleness about the man that somehow gave no offense. He sniffed loudly, patted his haunches as if trying to find a hanky, then, finding none, he sniffed again with relish. 'One thing I have learned is that which takes life can just as often return it. Stand back, would you please. Thank you so much. Now, let's see.'

Close up, it was his features, not his remarkable armour that was the most striking thing about him. He had the same long face and highly intelligent eyes that Pail and Frobisher shared, but there was an upturn at the corners of his mouth, a sort of perpetual good-humour that was one hundred percent Giff. Right at the back of the ground, standing next to a watchful Frobisher, Granny Avfeldig gasped.

'Tum di dum, pom p'pom, doodely dum …' He hummed under his breath, deftly removing Pail's helmet and punctured breastplate. He held Pail's wrist for a few moments. 'Jolly good!' he suddenly exclaimed very loudly, making several of the people closest to him jump. He turned to June. 'You have a fine, strong boy here, young lady. Does he eat plenty of fruit?'

'Wha-? Um …' June, who hadn't been called young lady in a couple of decades, was thrown. 'Yes, no … I'm not sure…' she glanced at her injured husband, who was being looked after by Mistress Moon. 'I suppose so …'

'Well either way, he should!' the old man glared around him good-naturedly. 'In fact, you all should!' He looked back at Pail, then across at what was left of Bane. 'Hmm, so you've been up at the Castle. I thought you would … sooner or later. These things can be very dangerous – particularly this one, if I remember rightly … *but* they have their uses.' He glanced around the assembled company and his eyes settled on Giff. 'Ah, you boy!' he said, 'you seem like a good strong lad … would you mind picking up that great big sword of his?'

'This one?' Giff took a reluctant step towards the bubbling remains of Bane.

'No, his other massive sword … of course *that* one. Yes, that's it … now pick it up … you'll need both hands, I daresay … *good*. Right, this is the tricky bit – and by the way, make sure you don't get any of that runny stuff on your armour, it's a devil to get out in the wash – now, my boy, have a dig around with the end of that thing where his heart should be.'

Giff hefted the sword as best he could and, using it like a lance, pushing it into what was left of Bane's torso. The viscous mass hissed and bubbled and Giff shuddered, half expecting Bane to rise up again for one last assault.

'That's right. Find anything hard?'

Giff's face was all concentration. 'No … actually wait!' He twisted the blade this way and that, then heaved it upwards with a slight grunt. For a moment it looked as if the sword was stuck fast but, as it finally wrenched free, something flicked out with it and landed in the mud. Something the size of a small grapefruit: something faceted and shiny.

Rainbeard (for no-one doubted by now who it was) seemed ecstatic. 'Well done, my boy! Well done! I don't think anyone here could have done better!' and, as he said this, he offered just the merest wink to Venn, before he leant down and gingerly picked Bane's ruby heart out of the black mud.

🍀

What happened next may have been a miracle – Terence, Granny Avfeldig and many others insisted for years after that it was. But Frobisher – and probably Pail, too, had he been awake at the time – would have had their doubts. Pail was already forming the opinion that one man's magic was just another's general knowledge. The everyday human ability to start fires, build warm houses, and live seemingly forever must have amazed the sheep in the village. But what Rainbeard did next always remained inexplicable to Pail, although he lived for a very long time and learned many marvellous things.

Carefully, with the gentleness that even his own mother would have struggled to match, he pressed the dark red gemstone to Pail's wound.

The effect was instantaneous. Utterly miraculous. All colour from the trees, the clearing sky, the warmth from the awakening earth; all of *Rainbeard's Spring* seemed to pour into Pail, who took a huge hiccoughing breath and promptly farted.

'Humph, yes, well,' said Rainbeard, 'that's one of the side effects … but you'll probably agree, very minor …'

'Not from where I'm standing,' someone said.

Rainbeard sniffed again, and for one fleeting moment looking terribly pleased with himself as Pail's bleeding stopped and his chest rose and fell evenly. Then he turned to June and Simon. 'Well! That's taken care of. He'll need plenty of rest etcetera, which I have no doubt he will ignore. And I've already mentioned fruit …'

Leaping up, June broke the habit of a lifetime and kissed

a complete stranger.

'Oh, no, no, dear girl, don't thank me, I've really got no time for all of that. If these chaps have been running about, I imagine the old place is going to need some attention. I'll need you again,' he pointed a bony finger at Giff. 'And you …' he pointed at Venn, 'appear to have a compound fracture of the right tibia and a possible dislocation of the knee cap, which I'll need to see up at the Castle. There should be enough lime and bandages to make a decent cast … might I trouble you for some further service, gentlemen?' And, at this, he looked directly for the first time at Frobisher, Sir Godfrey and Percival.

'But, of course.' Sir Godfrey gave a courtly bow.

Frobisher nodded sombrely. Percival grinned.

~:*Several weeks later...* :~

SIR GODFREY WAS HAVING a conversation with Venn as they took a turn around one of the ornamental gardens at the back of the Castle.

The three elderly knights had been invited to spend the summer in Four Frogs by Rainbeard – not having an awful lot to do at home, it was an invitation they had readily accepted. In his day, Rainbeard had been famous amongst the other knights in the kingdom, not just for being a bit of an eccentric but also for his hospitality.

And he didn't disappoint them – least of all Percival, who was visibly moved to tears of joy at the sight of Rainbeard's wine cellar. Giff had never seen a grown man cry and laugh at the same time.

Although the ancient knight was obviously very tired from his journey and his efforts with Pail, he insisted on giving them a guided tour on the first evening, after he had set Venn's broken leg. The first place they visited was deep within the deepest of all the cellars, a cave that was carved out of the solid rock below the Castle. Rainbeard fussed about for a few minutes and eventually found what he was looking for – a sort of crystal panel embedded in a slab of limestone. Upon the crystal panel there were a series of numbers and symbols that he tapped several times in a sequence. Nothing happened for a few moments, then there was a loud grinding of stone against stone as the walls seemed to move inwards. Copious amounts of dust shot out from newly appeared cracks in the rock, all of which eventually settled to reveal an open door way and a room containing two coffers.

'Ah! Good,' said Rainbeard, looking slightly surprised, as if he hadn't really expected it to work. He turned to Giff, who was still coughing. 'If you wouldn't mind opening the one on the left, it should be full of gold. However, it's in everyone's best interests if you don't touch the other one, it's full of spiders or snakes … or it may explode – I can't really remember. In any case, it's some sort of booby trap. Talking of which, I'll have to see that they're all removed elsewhere, now that you're all going to be staying here.'

'Shheeesh,' said Giff, as he heaved off the lid, suddenly filling the room with a radiant amber glow. 'OK, so what do you want me to do with all this?'

Rainbeard rolled his eyes at Percival, who felt it necessary to state, 'He grows on you.'

'Kids these days,' Rainbeard muttered, and then more loudly, 'I would have thought that was obvious: fill your pockets up with as much as you can carry, then go down to the village and invite everyone here for first thing tomorrow … we've got a lot of cleaning up to do and I can't be bothered to do it all myself. *Then* take half a dozen of your most reliable lads and buy as much food as you can from the villages nearby, and get some livestock, too – chickens, goats and …' he waved his hand impatiently, already striding back out of the cellar as the vault doors closed of their own accord, '… we'll need some sheep, plenty of sheep.'

The following two months weeks passed in a welter of activity. It was now high summer and since the villagers had all been invited to live up at the Castle, leaving the village below effectively abandoned, the place had changed out of all recognition. The stockade had been burned and the broken cottages pulled down for timber, which was then used to build better houses with beautiful views in the great courtyard within the castle walls. The top of the hill was now a hive of daily activity.

Rainbeard seemed to spend most of his mornings marching about the place energetically; nodding approvingly at the comfortable new thatched cottages that were being built; offering suspect and highly changeable advice on animals in general and sheep specifically; and generally being a good-humoured pain in the neck. After a large lunch, when Percival would take himself off for a snooze, he, Frobisher and the recovering Pail, would lock themselves away in the study at the top of the Fast Tower and stay there until suppertime discussing matters of invention and who knows what.

One of the very first things they had done was to bring the remains of the Iron Knights up to the Castle. Bludge and Squawk were partially reassembled. As for Bane, one moonless night, all three had taken the remains to a dark part of the forest and buried them there, sealed in a lead casket.

'Can we make them work again then?' Pail asked Rainbeard one afternoon, as he gazed at the iron cadaver of Squawk.

'I'm surprised you ask.'

Pail smiled slightly in response. Since his recovery, he had seemed quieter, but somehow poised, more sure of himself. Even Frobisher treated him more like an equal every day. He rapped his knuckles on the spiked iron head. 'Only after we cure whatever it is that caused them to behave like that, of course,' he added.

'Well,' Rainbeard replied, after a moment's hesitation, 'I'm not sure that's possible. I have learned that you cannot always change the nature of a mere machine. What it was built for.' Then he shrugged, 'but I always say that nothing's impossible, so perhaps *you* can … perhaps you'll find a way, one day … you know, I think they'd make fantastic guards.'

❧

Whatever studies and experiments they got up to, Sir Godfrey seemed oddly disapproving of the whole thing. He did all he could to avoid the Fast Tower with its Harp Staircase. And Venn, too, who had seen enough technical wizardry to last at least a couple of lifetimes, fell into the habit of accompanying Sir Godfrey on his short walks round the gardens on the south side of the Castle. Exercise was good for his leg, according to Rainbeard.

As a kindly old knight who took an interest in others, Sir Godfrey hadn't failed to notice that Venn and Stirn were still distant with one another. Stirn seemed to have suffered more than most during the Iron Knight's reign of terror and certainly looked far older than his fifty-five years. He still did his best to put in a full day's work and, although the villagers had begun to look upon Venn as a sort of natural heir to the Headman, Stirn was still treated with respect. This sharing of roles should have brought the father and son closer – instead, as the summer progressed, they spoke less and less and never directly to one another, more often addressing their questions through Maisy, or Sir Godfrey himself.

Sir Godfrey was sensitive enough to guess that the distance was born from the forced separation – at an age when Venn had most needed a father. It goes without saying that he was then clever enough to deduce that two leaders who didn't talk would cause problem in the village later on.

He'd thought about it carefully for a while and decided

that the direct approach was best.

'You must make your peace with your father.'

Venn, walking with his usual slight limp next to Sir Godfrey, stiffened somewhat but said nothing immediately. Thoughts crowded the silence, slowly filling it up, until Venn eventually blurted out. 'It's not that simple.'

'Oh, but it is. You both love each other, do you not?' Venn paused, as if the question surprised him but then nodded emphatically.

'Yes, of course we do. But …'

'Hmm?'

'But, whenever I talk to him, we argue. When I talk to you it's … easy.'

Godfrey smiled kindly. 'It's easy because I am not your father. You are at an age when all sons question what their parents, particularly their fathers, stand for. But you also missed out on the middle years. The good years, when the bond between you both would have been forged and made unbreakable.'

'He sent us away.'

'For your own good – you know that, so let's have no false hurt. It was a terrible situation and it was not,' Sir Godfrey made a waving motion, silencing Venn who looked agitated, 'your fault in the least. It was no-one's fault, just a terrible thing that happened and your father … your parents did what they thought best – to protect you.'

Venn's years spent with Sir Godfrey and Lady Elspeth had made him independent, far more so than anyone at the age of fifteen should be, but he was also naturally given to helping others. With this in mind, Sir Godfrey played his master card.

'Your parents need you now.'

This statement brought Venn up short, his healing leg scuffing the fine white gravel on the path.

'Why do you say that?'

'Simply because it is true. You are no longer a child and your parents are no longer young. All too soon in life the roles are reversed.' And Sir Godfrey left it at that.

The following evening, there was a great feast in the courtyard, it being still warm enough to eat outside, although summer was now on the wane. Trestle tables lined the length of the paved area where children played and a great bonfire crackled – spitting orange sparks up into the sky where they whirled, like reddish fireflies dancing around the silver stars.

But, Giff is right – good food is for eating, not talking about – so I won't bore you with details of what they ate: the hot glazed porks, mountains of cold beef, steaming dumplings, roast venison and treacle puddings you could drown in.

In part, the feast was a celebration of what they had all achieved over the summer: the Iron Knights beaten and the new village that had been built, nestled safe within the Castle walls. But it was also an opportunity to say farewell and give thanks to the knights, Lord Frobisher, Sir Godfrey and Percival Locke who were leaving the next day, to return to their own castles.

Venn, instead of sitting at the top table with Giff and Pail, had gone over to where his parents were sitting, next to Farn and Didee. Somewhat shyly, he had asked Farn to move along the bench so he could place himself next to his father. As he slid along the bench, Stirn had hesitantly placed a hand on Venn's shoulder. No more than this.

But it was noted by Sir Godfrey, who took a big swig of wine and felt quite pleased with himself.

Towards the end of the fourth course (after the clear soup, cold meats, roasts and first round of chocolate puddings, none of which I have any intention of describing in detail) there was a natural lull in the conversation.

Rainbeard took this as his cue to stand up.

He cleared his throat once or twice, which made the people eating nearest stop talking and eating, then rapped his bony knuckles on the wooden table for wider attention. For a minute or so, there were so many people telling other people to be quiet that the noise level actually increased but, bit by bit, the hubbub died down again and, eventually, he began.

'Good people, *kind* people of Four Frogs who have endured so much these last few years and worked so hard to rebuild what was broken, I raise my goblet of wine to you, to toast your endurance and your bravery!'

There was a huge cheer.

'And secondly, I recharge and raise this gaudy vessel again, to honour these gentle knights,' he smiled at Frobisher, Godfrey and Percival. 'Who took three boys into their homes, who looked after and cared for them out of nothing but decency and a desire to do the right thing and who,' he paused as the diners gave another cheer, '... who then had the courage to leave their homes, risking their lives to lend their assistance just when it was needed most.'

More loud cheering: Frobisher bowed slightly stiffly at Rainbeard, then at the rows of people; Sir Godfrey blushed; and Percival beamed so broadly and for so long it looked like his face was stuck.

Finally, Rainbeard raised his glass a third time, motioning with his free hand, once again, for silence.

'And lastly, though by no means *leastly*, would you join me in saluting the achievements of three young men who, despite making a mistake, suffered the consequences with a resilience and with humility worthy of any knight. Three young boys from ordinary homes, who had the courage and the honour to return to Four Frogs and put right what was so wrong, although it nearly cost them their lives.' He stopped and looked at his hands. 'You know, I have been thinking these last few weeks and have come to several decisions. First of all, as your Lord – and quite without heir – this kingdom of England, so just and so gracious, permits me to elevate these fine young men to the rank of knight.'

Rainbeard looked up and paused for a few moments, to allow his twinkling eyes to fully take in the effect of this announcement. Then he went on in a much louder, more strident voice, easily drowning the gasps of amazement around the long dining tables.

'From this day forth, as the Lord of this Castle, I proclaim that Venn, Pail and Giff will each be inheritor of an equal share of this proud edifice and its dominions, when I am one day gone from this world! And I further declare that this inheritance be passed down, when they reach the age of fifty, to three others who best show the strength of character and courage they have displayed. So, without further ado, arise Sir Venn, Sir Pail and Sir Giff of Four Frogs!'

It took a few moments for the titles to sink in and then the entire place erupted. More wine was brought out of the cellars, the fire was piled high with thick wedges of timber, Soozie Brick made a grab for Giff and the music started.

Amidst all the noise of happy celebrations, including some raucous singing and some very questionable dancing, it was only the watchful Pail who noticed someone quietly slip away.

~: Farewell :~

AWAY FROM THE CASTLE, the night was still. Not a lick of air disturbed the trees around the archway and hardly any light penetrated the thick canopy. Rainbeard stopped but didn't turn. 'I know you are there, young Pail. Or I should really say, *Sir* Pail now.'

'You're leaving.'

'Yes, it would appear that I am. Would you care to accompany me through the forest? An old man, alone, may need protection on a dark night like this.' Pail seriously doubted this, but he remained silent as he fell into step with Rainbeard who walked surprisingly fast, considering how dark it was. 'What will your motto be, then? All knights do need one, you know.'

They were passing under the arch where Pail, Venn and Giff had paused before going up the hill to the castle, all those years ago. Rainbeard pointed at the inscription in Greek. "*Το μήλο κάτω απ' τη μηλιά θα πέσει.*" He said in the strange tongue. 'Do you know what the Greek means?'

'The apple does not fall far from the tree,' said Pail without pausing. He'd looked it up.

Rainbeard looked dutifully impressed. 'Quite so, quite so! And do you agree? Can people change their birth?'

Pail thought about it. 'I think what it is saying is wrong,' he said slowly. 'If they really want to, anyone can transform, look at …' and he stopped, not wanted to sound boastful.

'That's alright. You three friends changed because you had to and you should take credit for that. But never forget, we're not just who we make of ourselves. Another proverb says that *no man is an island*, and this is also true. In fact, the two proverbs should go together on that arch … I must see to that one day – or perhaps you could.' Rainbeard looked at his young companion, his eyes intense in the moonlight. 'The decency in you, the sense of honour that told all of you that you must come back and put things right, came from your parents. They brought you up well and for that they should be proud and you grateful.' Rainbeard turned and started to march down the path, retracing the boys' steps to the clearing where it all began. 'So what's it to be then? Your motto?'

Pail made a show of thinking about it but his mind was already made up.

'*Honos, amicitia, fides*,' he said.

'*Honour, friendship and loyalty*,' Rainbeard nodded, 'simple but solid virtues all … yes, I like that.'

'Where are you going?' Pail knew that it was none of his business but he'd had a couple of glasses of wine, and he felt brave enough to ask.

Rainbeard stopped as if considering the question for the first time. 'Well, I hadn't really thought about any real destination, but summer is drawing to a close, so I imagine south. Italy, perhaps – I haven't been to Rome for a lifetime.'

'How old are you, sir?'

'Ha! *My*, we are feeling bold tonight.' The question seemed to amuse him rather than offend. 'To tell you the truth, I stopped counting when I reached eighty, and that was a long time ago.' Pail thought of all the things they had discussed up at the top of the Fast Tower. Rainbeard seemed to read his thoughts. 'You have all your life ahead of you, Pail, you don't need an old man like me hanging about the place. Cramp your style.'

Pail nodded, although he didn't agree – he had only known the old man for a few weeks but he felt close to tears at his departure. He was glad it was dark. 'Are you coming back?'

Rainbeard shrugged. 'Yes, perhaps. I usually seem to know when I'm needed.'

They had come to the edge of the village square where Rainbeard's mount, Storm, was waiting patiently, tied to the old oak where his armour also lay in a neat pile beside two saddlebags. And next to those stood Frobisher, holding his own horse. He must have taken the main road to have got there before them.

'Ah, my travelling companion!' Rainbeard seemed even more full of life than usual, exuding cheerfulness.

'My Lord,' said Frobisher, who seemed momentarily surprised to see Pail. 'Pail. I am glad you are here. I am returning in a year, in case you were wondering. I didn't want to leave without saying goodbye properly, but Rainbeard here wanted no fuss.'

'I don't mind. Now I have the chance to say thank you, sir – thank you for everything.' Pail was happier than ever that he had followed.

'Well Frobisher, young Pail here has one more question to ask of me before we get on our way.' Rainbeard winked at Pail. 'He also thinks we should go to Rome, then perhaps Alexandria, have a look at the library there – over 75,000 scrolls, don't you know?'

And it was true, Pail did have something to ask, but he didn't know which words to use. He'd almost asked a few times over the long summer but the question somehow seemed impertinent. He wouldn't have dared now, if it hadn't been for Rainbeard somehow guessing that something was on his mind. So this was it. He watched Rainbeard expertly strap on his armour and load his other belongings onto Storm before finally blurting it out.

'How did you do it ... bring me back to life ... it makes

no sense? And I don't really understand how Bane worked, what made him how he was. When he died, why didn't I, like the book said I must?'

The night suddenly seemed to become more still, as if the creatures in the forest had stopped what they were doing to hear Rainbeard's answer. Even Frobisher leaned forward.

Rainbeard tightened the last strap and turned around. He smiled softly and chuckled. 'I hope you don't think I made those monstrous things!' He shook his head. 'No, they were found in the bowels of the castle, in the bedrock that makes up the foundations. I only discovered them, quite by chance in fact, when I was a young man. I had just inherited the land and was having the castle built. That cave I was storing the gold in and the crystal panel that worked the door was what housed them. Took me weeks to work out how to open it. I just got them working – rather like you! But I also had that book, and I was a little older and wiser, so I took some precautions before I woke them. They were never allowed to exercise their real strength, which is why the tall one always hated me.

'I daresay I shouldn't have left them lying around, but I always find that people, especially small boys, will always find something dangerous to do, however much you try and keep them out of harm's way. This has been a learning experience for us all, I daresay!'

Pail could hardly believe his ears. 'But I still don't know how they worked – especially Bane. How did the ruby in his heart save me? Venn says I died!'

Rainbeard tugged at his white beard and sighed. 'One reason why I never trusted those mechanical monsters was that, although I managed to get them going, I never fully understood how I did it. As for curing you, all I know is that it works. That was good enough for me at the time and it'll have to do for you now. Sometimes in life, you have to be content with not grasping how something works and just be thankful that it does – it's what keeps it interesting. I know the sun rises in the morning but I've absolutely no idea how.' He looked at Pail. 'I suppose you did really die, just like the book said you would, but the ruby in his chest had your blood – you made him live and it still contained enough of your life to revive you. I daresay that if I'd come along a few minutes later, then I would have been too late!' He climbed onto Storm. 'But like I say, I always seem to know when I'm needed. And – I might add – when I'm just getting in the way! So goodbye and best of luck … and do try not to break anything when I'm gone.'

'Er, yes,' said Pail, feeling sad but understanding their reasons for leaving. 'OK.'

And with that, Pail watched them go, leading their horses down the track, out of Four Frogs. He stayed there for a very long time, watching their slowly moving shadows gradually blend into the darkness.

When the sound of their footsteps had faded to nothing, he turned and walked back to the Castle.

~: The End :~

the story of

~: *Four Frogs* :~

THERE ARE MANY STORIES relating to the strange, isolated village known as Four Frogs. Some involve the Iron Knights, Rainbeard and the three friends: Venn, Pail and Giff. Others do not. However, in this modern day and age, no one is exactly sure where the village once lay – or indeed, if it were not a sort of mish-mash of several villages up and down the country with a similar name.

Opinions also differ as to how the village came by its name. The most obvious explanation (and thus the most boring) is that it was an anglicised version of the words *Forge Frogg* – the forge of a blacksmith called Frogg. However, the most far-fetched and therefore interesting explanation goes something like this:

❧

There were once four young sons of a powerful and very rich monarch.

Not only was their father absolutely loaded, but he also enjoyed rude health well into his eighties, which meant that he was able to run his kingdom without any help from his children. Unfortunately, this also meant that the four princes grew up idle, vain and rather spoiled. Each passed his time indulging in one daft activity after the other: organising elaborate balls; hunting for rare beasts that hid in the darkest forests; buying things they didn't need; and wearing ridiculous clothes. You know – the usual stuff.

Their sole preoccupation in life – the only thing, in fact, that really interested any of them – was competing with their siblings over who had the finest things. One prince chose a lovely spot in a forest that had magnificent views over the rolling countryside for miles, reaching all the way to the sea, and immediately ordered that every oak, ash and elm be hacked down to make way for a castle. Another had a great tower constructed of rare marble that had been shipped all the way from Rome. Not a soul was allowed inside, lest they trailed any mud onto the cream and pink floors. The youngest drank far too much wine one day and ordered *his* entire castle to be made of cake.

The princes were not especially cruel but their stupidity was such that, little by little, they were laying waste the kingdom as efficiently as any marauding army. As the money ran out, their subjects began to go hungry and get sick. Crops failed for lack of decent seed and cattle died because they were not allowed to feed off the grass that the princes liked to grow high – simply because they preferred the look of fields that way.

In those far-off days, nitwits of royal blood were considered right, even when they were completely in the wrong, so the King and his people could do nothing but sit by and await their doom.

✿

Then, out of the blue, riding on the back of a small, vile-tempered donkey, their prayers were answered in the form of a wandering witch.

As she travelled the main road through the kingdom on her way to the castle, the witch took a long, considered look around at the bony cattle, the small, unhappy children and the absurd confectionary castle that, by now, was covered in insects of every description. And her eyes narrowed.

She carried on up the hill, not stopping until she got to

the portcullis of the King's castle, where the four princes still lived with their parents.

'What do you want, *Crone*?' asked the Master-at-Arms. But he kept his distance because … well, because you never know with witches, even if you've got two feet of oak between you and them.

'I wish to see these four great princes I have heard so much about,' she replied. 'I have a totally amazing gift for them.'

'They want for nothing, those princes,' said the Master-at-Arms with some feeling. 'So be on your way.' He glanced past her. 'And could you tell your donkey to stop doing that. I've only just had those cobbles scrubbed.' But the witch wasn't going anywhere.

''Tis a gift that can't be bought with mere gold,' she replied levelly. 'And they will be angry if you turn me away and they miss out on this great thing I have for them. I may well end up giving it to other, less deserving princes.' The Master-at-Arms thought about it and shrugged. Won't harm to ask, he thought.

'Wait here!' he barked, disappearing for a few minutes.

When he came back, he was carrying a huge key. 'OK,' he said, 'you can come in, but leave your ass here.'

'Rightyho!' replied the witch cheerfully as the man opened the door, 'thankee kindly.' And in she tripped.

❧

The princes' Audience Room looked like a bomb had gone off in the make-up department of a particularly gaudy shop.

At the far end of the chamber, the four princes entered from four different, highly decorated doors and placed their royal behinds on four equally preposterous-looking thrones.

'Speak, oh wrinkly one!' said the eldest after a bit.

'Yes, what have you got for us, peasant biddy?'

As you have probably worked out, none of them had met a witch before and they had no idea the danger they were in.

'She smells of donkey, I think I'm going to expire!' exclaimed the youngest rather loudly, bringing a lavender-scented hanky to his long nose.

The witch's eyes narrowed for a second time.

'Ooooh, yer royal 'ighnesses,' she said, playing her part perfectly. 'Oooh! Oi'm soo grateful that yous agreed to see me – an 'umble owld wandering gypsy. Begging yer pardon, and youz must be so busy with running this beautiful kingdom, a lookin' aftir yer loyal subjects …' The princes glanced at each other and shrugged, '… but I 'as a rare gift to bestow on each of youz, simply to gain yer royal favour …' she paused and eyed them. The princes may have been vain and stupid in many respects, but they had a native cunning, derived from a love of cold cash, '… and in exchange – pr'haps – for a few small pennies …' she added hastily.

This last remark drew sly smiles from the four princes. They were on familiar ground now.

'And what is this gift?' said the second youngest, who had been silent up until now. The witch bowed as low as she could and thought of the skinny, unhappy looking children, the dead livestock and the foolish buildings.

'Princes you may be, but KINGS is better! When you hand over the pennies, I will rub my magic turnip,' at this she whipped out a muddy-looking vegetable and waved it about. 'And you will each become king of all you survey in an instant. The finest coat of emerald you will wear and you will never have need for another garment. You will walk on land but be able to hunt underwater. And each of you will have a great floating palace to live in … a fine singing voice to serenade the very stars to tears and strength … why, I daresay you would be able to leap fifteen times your height!'

To the princes, this sounded so enticing that none of them noticed she'd just lost her accent. But the second youngest, who had been silent up until this point and who was also possibly the brightest, piped up.

'And should we choose, how would we break this enchantment?'

The witch quickly reverted to character. 'Oh, 'tis as easy as one, two, three … not that I can imagine youz would ever want ter!'

'So. How?' The prince could be a stickler, it has to be said.

'Why, just ask a princess to kiss you.'

'Ha! Then I shall do it!' announced the oldest, who could hardly wait. He'd yet to meet a princess who didn't want to kiss him – though personally he couldn't see the point.

'And so shall I!'

'And I!' There was a pause, whilst the fourth prince considered things.

'Oh, well,' he said eventually, feigning boredom, 'why not?'

So, waving her turnip (which really was magic) the witch promptly turned all four vain princes into four very surprised frogs.

***

And that's how they stayed. When the King realised that there was very little chance of them turning back into idle young men of their own accord, he had a pond made for each in a tiny hidden village that nestled in the heart of his kingdom, hidden in its own valley. Each pond had its own log and a sign that read, *No princesses!*

And that is how the kingdom was saved and how the village of Four Frogs got its unusual name.

***